J.H. Riddel

Far above Rubies

Vol. 2

J.H. Riddel

Far above Rubies
Vol. 2

ISBN/EAN: 9783337225933

Printed in Europe, USA, Canada, Australia, Japan

Cover: Foto ©Andreas Hilbeck / pixelio.de

More available books at **www.hansebooks.com**

FAR ABOVE RUBIES.

A Novel.

BY

Mrs. J. H. RIDDELL,

AUTHOR OF "GEORGE GEITH," "CITY AND SUBURB," "TOO MUCH ALONE,"
"THE RACE FOR WEALTH," ETC., ETC.

IN THREE VOLUMES.

VOL. II.

LONDON:

TINSLEY BROTHERS, CATHERINE STREET, STRAND.

1867.

LONDON: PRINTED BY WILLIAM CLOWES AND SONS, STAMFORD STREET
AND CHARING CROSS.

CONTENTS OF VOL. II.

iv CONTENTS.

CHAPTER VIII.

CHAPTER IX.

CHAPTER X.

CHAPTER XI.

CHAPTER XII.

FAR ABOVE RUBIES.

CHAPTER I.

AMIDST the anxieties of making salads, the desire to convert Heather from the evils and dangers of English cookery, skirmishes with Mrs. Ormson, criticisms on Bessie, and the personal enjoyment of such luxuries as ripe fruit, coffee of her own manufacture, chocolate and claret *ad libitum*, Miss Hope by no means forgot Mr. Black's commercial scheme, and the efforts she felt confident he was making to induce Arthur to embark in it with him.

A woman sharp and clever enough in her genera-tion, she was yet no match, either in sharpness or cleverness, for Mr. Black. If she knew a few things

VOL. II.   B

about him, he "was up," so he phrased it, "to two or three of her moves," and could turn the tables on her, when she tried his temper, as is often the wise fashion of her sex, a little too much.

The very first morning she opened fire upon him, the promoter informed Arthur, he "knew what the old lady was up to."

This was the peculiarly diplomatic manner in which Miss Hope, finding that Heather inclined to do nothing, commenced her operations.

The time was breakfast; scene, the dining-room at Berrie Down, with all the windows open; actors, Miss Hope and Mr. Black; interested spectators, the family and visitors generally.

"Pray," began the spinster, coquetting, as she spoke, with a peach which might have been grown in Eden, it looked so fresh and tempting; "pray, Mr. Black, can you tell me of a good investment for a small sum of money?"

Across the table Mr. Black looked at her, with a merry twinkle in his eyes; then he answered,—

"Yes, the Three per Cents."

"But my friend would not be satisfied with three per cent.," said Miss Hope.

"A mortgage, or some good freehold estate, might suit her then," suggested Mr. Black.

"I did not say it was a lady, so far as I am aware," remarked Miss Hope.

"No; but I concluded no man would ask a lady friend to make such inquiries for him," explained her antagonist. "She might get four, or even four and a half, and still be safe enough."

"But what is four and a half?" observed Miss Hope.

"Four pounds ten shillings per cent. per annum," answered Mr. Black, at which reply Arthur laughed.

"You won't make much of him, aunt," he said; "you cannot get him to advise an unsafe investment."

For a moment Miss Hope turned towards her nephew, evidently meditating an attack on him. Changing her mind, however, she addressed herself to Mr. Black once more.

"But there is more surely than four and a half per cent. to be had now-a-days, is there not; in some of those great companies, for instance?"

"All swindles, ma'am," declared the promoter. "Should not advise you, or at least your friend, to have anything to do with them. In the companies that are *bona fide*, all the shares are snapped up before the project is well before the public. Whenever you hear of shares going a-begging, depend upon it the whole concern is rotten."

"You are an authority in such matters?" she suggested.

"Not a better authority than Miss Hope," replied Mr. Black, gallantly.

"What do you mean; do you think I know anything about investments?" she asked.

"I have heard that either you or some friend of yours does," he answered. "I have heard of very good ventures you have made,—of shares sold in the nick of time, and bought wisely, and at a very low figure."

"I assure you, Mr. Black, you have been misinformed," said the spinster, eagerly; "all my money is sunk in a life annuity."

"Which, no doubt, ma'am, you purchased on as favourable terms as those shares in the Great Britain and Ireland Canal Company."

"Then you *had* to do with that!" exclaimed Miss Hope, setting down her claret-glass with most unladylike vehemence, and looking at the promoter as though he were a culprit caught in the very act. "I always thought that was one of your schemes; but never felt sure of it till now."

"It is not wise to be too sure of anything," Mr. Black answered. "I had nothing, as it happened, to do with the Great Britain and Ireland Canal Company. If I had, perhaps you might not have lost by your shares; but a man I know, a confoundedly clever fellow, got rid of his •the day before the smash came, and it was he who told me you had got your fingers burnt. Your friend, Mr. Pembroke, did not advise you with his customary caution there, Miss Hope."

"Mr. Pembroke had nothing to do with the matter," said Miss Hope, angrily; "and how you happen to be so well acquainted with my private affairs is a mystery to me. I do not consider such prying gentlemanly. I do not know what may be thought of such conduct among business people, Mr. Black, but in a different circle——"

"I thought it was of business we were talking," interrupted the promoter, "of affairs which were strictly commercial. The moment any one goes on the market, Miss Hope, either personally or by deputy, that moment he or she becomes public property. I never pretended to be a gentleman; but I do not think I would go prying into my neighbour's secret concerns for all that, any more than you would do," he added, significantly.

Almost involuntarily Heather's eyes sought Miss Hope's face at this statement, and under Mrs. Dudley's look the spinster turned redder even than she had done at the conclusion of Mr. Black's speech.

"I am perfectly incapable of impertinent or undue meddling in any person's concerns," she said. "Thank God, curiosity is a feeling that I was born without."

"Then you ought to be sent to the South Kensington Museum," remarked Mr. Black.

"Don't you think, aunt, that is going a little too far ?" inquired Arthur.

"Miss Hope only meant that she had no curiosity about indifferent subjects," put in Mrs. Black, as usual making matters worse by trying to mend them.

"Miss Hope meant no such thing," snapped that lady. "I meant precisely what I said; that I have no curiosity, and that I never had any."

"Not even to see unfinished pictures and statues in course of chiselling," suggested Mrs. Ormson.

"I do not think Miss Hope has any undue curiosity," said Heather ; "at least, I know she has not nearly so much as I. It interests me to know the name, and occupation, and worldly means, even, of Dora Scrotter's lover down at the mill. In the country one learns to be inquisitive about one's neighbours. There is so little excitement or amusement, that every piece of gossip is seized on eagerly."

"You dear Heather, as if you were a gossip !" exclaimed Bessie.

"That is just what I say about the country," remarked Mr. Black; "life stagnates here; you should come to London, Mrs. Dudley; come and bring the girls, and we will take you about. There are lots of rooms in Stanley Crescent crying out for some one to come and occupy them. Persuade your husband to give himself a holiday whenever the crops are in; you have never paid us a visit yet, and I call it mean."

"We should be only too delighted if you would come," murmured Mrs. Black.

"Well, all *I* can say is," remarked Miss Hope,

"that if I had such a place as Berrie Down, I would never leave it."

"Not even to go abroad?" asked Mrs. Ormson.

"Not even to go abroad," answered Miss Hope, deliberately—an assertion which took every one so much by surprise, that no person disputed its truthfulness; not even Arthur, who, feeling his aunt's words were intended as a useful moral lesson for him, longed to argue the matter out with her, and say he should go to London, or stay at Berrie Down, or take a still longer journey if it pleased him to do so, without consulting any one in the matter.

"You would like greatly to have my nephew staying in Stanley Crescent?" Miss Hope said to Mrs. Black later on in the course of the same day.

"I should *greatly*," answered the promoter, and thus war was declared between them; and from that day forth Miss Hope began unintentionally playing into her enemy's hands.

"Take care what you are about with that man, Arthur," she entreated.

"My dear aunt, I am much obliged to you for your kindness, but I believe I can manage my own affairs," he returned.

" Heather, you must speak to Arthur," she then declared ; "if you do not speak, you will one day repent your weakness."

" But I am afraid of vexing him," Mrs. Dudley objected.

" Vex, nonsense ; better vex him than lose every sixpence you have in the world."

" Do you think my speaking likely to do any good ?"

" It cannot do any harm ;" and thus exhorted, Heather inquired,—

" Have you any intention, Arthur, of—of going into business ?"

" Business," he repeated ; " what in the world put such an idea as that into your mind ?"

" You and Mr. Black are always talking together."

" And you object to our talking ?"

" No ; only I love Berrie Down, Arthur."

" Which my aunt thinks I am in danger of losing ; is that it, Heather ? No, I won't lose Berrie Down, nor beggar you and the children. Does that content you ?"

" Yes, Arthur ;" and she put her arm round his neck, and kissed him ; and he, in return, kissed her, grateful, perhaps, for a wife whom so little confidence satisfied, or at least silenced; and who was as grateful for a kind word, for a loving look, as many a woman for the devotion of a life.

In those days, Arthur Dudley was a much more agreeable individual than he had seemed for many a year previously.

He was gayer, brighter, kindlier. He refrained from grumbling, and ceased to recite the benefits he had conferred upon his family.

There had come a summer to his winter, and in the bright sunshine all the good plants that were formerly hidden under the snows of adversity, put forth and blossomed into flower.

For such a change, could Heather be otherwise than thankful? Did not every creature about the house—every man, woman, and child, and even the very dumb animals—feel happier and better because the head of the family, believing fortune was coming towards him, looked out over the world with different eyes, and thought there was at last good to be found in it?

The labourers worked more willingly; the very cattle seemed to thrive better; the dogs, forgivingly forgetful that their master had been wont to repulse their demonstrations of affections with an angry, "Get off, will you!" came bounding towards him over the meadows and across the yard. They were so pleased with the notice he took of them in those days, that they lost their heads and made themselves perfectly ridiculous with their rejoicings and gambolings. They rolled each other over on the grass, and barked and worried each his companion in the friendliest manner possible. When Arthur entered the room, Muff, Lally's dearly beloved and much-enduring kitten, now kept her position, instead of walking off gravely shaking her hind legs at him as she went. He had been wont to kick her also out of the way, but now he did not disdain to look when Bessie held the saucer of milk for which she had taught Muff to beg.

Even Jinny, the ill-conditioned goat, came in for her share of the universal sunshine; while as for Heather, she basked in it. Had it not been for Miss Hope's eternal warnings, she would have forgotten her anxieties; ay, even the unpromising page of her own life which had been suddenly opened for her inspection.

Arthur was happy; and she is but a poor wife to whom the sight of her husband's happiness does not bring rejoicing also! As for Lally, a new leaf in her book also was turned over. One day she came in to her mother—hot, breathless, excited—exclaiming, " Lally's been to the mill, and Mr. Scrotter gave her two—beau—ful bantams!"

" Who went with you to the mill, my pet ?" asked Heather; little expecting, however, to hear Lally say in reply,—

" Pa tooked me; and pa says, when Lally's a big girl she shall have a nicer pony than Jack to ride, and that he'll go out with her. Pa says it!" and Lally stood and looked at her mother as though expecting Heather to make an immediate memorandum of these remarkable words.

Ah! Heaven, how the poor Squire built his castles and furnished them in that glorious summer weather; in what a fairy edifice he lived; through what rose-coloured glass he surveyed his future life! How different everything looked; how changed he felt; how swiftly the stream of his existence flowed by! He was galloping on to fortune, and he never thought of the chance of fall or accident by the way. He believed in his steed, and the idea of stumbling or breaking down never occurred to him. He was in for it now; he had—as Mr. Black said to himself at the conclusion of their first actual conversation on the subject—"tasted blood;" and till the game was hunted down, Arthur was never likely to look back.

Besides, there was such perpetual excitement about the matter. Letters arrived, letters were answered, advertisements were drawn up, a prospectus had to be written. Post time became a longed-for hour at Berrie Down.

There was something to do, something to expect; the monotony of that country existence was broken up. Life at the Hollow, all at once, ceased to be mere vegetation. For himself the Squire never could have made an object and a purpose; but here, constantly at his right hand, was a man full of energy and expedients—a man who had confidence both in himself and in his project; who, pulling away with might and main towards opulence and success, was kind enough to take Arthur Dudley as a passenger in the same boat, and amuse him, as they rowed along, with descriptions of that fair land whither they were journeying.

Many a wiser person than Arthur Dudley has been led away by much more delusive prospects of fortune than those concerning which Mr. Black waxed daily more and more eloquent.

Besides, the mere fact of having anything actually to do—"anything to get up for," so Mr. Black put the matter — proved an agreeable variety to the Squire.

He was not yet old enough to prefer repose to action, to dislike change, to distrust novelties; and there can be no question but that the brisk confidence of Mr. Black's ideas—the sharp decision of Mr. Black's manner, seemed a pleasant variety to a man who had for years and years been droning through life, wandering over the fields with his hands in his pockets, grumbling at his labourers, lamenting concerning his inferior crops, and his cattle that would not grow beef fast enough.

Other trifles also conspired to gratify him at this time; such trifles as a man must have lived very quietly and very economically even to notice. But then it was many a long day since Arthur had lived otherwise than quietly and economically, and for that' reason one or two journeys taken to town about this period with Mr. Black—when the pair went about London regardless of expense, rushed from one end of town to the other in hansoms, kept cabs waiting for them without a thought of the ultimate cost; tipped footmen, porters, watermen; took trains from all parts of London for all suburbs and country districts that could be mentioned; treated subordinates to wonderful luncheons, or else had them up for dinner to Stanley Crescent, and went with them afterwards to the play—made a curious impression on the mind of a man who had hitherto looked conscientiously at a sovereign before spending it; who had almost ever since he left college travelled second-class, affected omnibuses, shunned staying in great houses on account of needful gratuities, and generally pinched himself as much as an honest gentleman, left but with a small property and many incumbrances, was likely to do.

Of course, this recital of scraping, careful, unexciting poverty must prove as wearisome and unendurable in a book as the reality does, when your neighbour (a person to be shunned) says he has to count his sixpences carefully and walk to the station for the sake of his family. The least said is soonest mended in such cases, no doubt; and the terrible economics poor Squire Dudley had been guilty of are now reluctantly named only to render intelligible the reason why rattling about London, in company with Mr. Black, seemed to him pleasant by contrast.

To be sure—and this is really the singular part of the business—what was spent came out of Arthur's pocket. Various heads of cattle speedily followed Nellie, and the money they yielded was distributed by Mr. Black with no niggardly hand.

He knew the means by which to float a company; he believed that the way to every man's heart was through the palm of his right hand.

Mesmerism, he said, was a round-about way of putting yourself *en rapport* with any one, in comparison to slipping a sovereign between his fingers.

Further, to get up other people's steam, it is necessary, first, to raise your own; and Mr. Black held, and held truly, that there is no easier way of doing this than to rush from office to office, from station to bank, from bank to private house, all at express speed.

"This is how we live," he was wont to say to Arthur Dudley; and, on the whole, the Squire thought such a way of living far from disagreeable.

They did not ask or want money from anyone, I pray you recollect.   The great ship was still on the stocks; there had not occurred a single hitch in the business; it was all fair weather work, so far, at least, as Arthur could see; all like ordering goods and writing cheques; giving employment and paying cash; and it never occurred to the Squire that there could be another side to the picture; that sometimes business assumed the form of selling goods, and asking for payment.   He was but a novice, and believed implicitly their ship would glide smoothly into the water; that she would carry a good cargo; that the profits on her freight would be enormous; that the passengers would all have a fair voyage, and agree well by the way; that there would be plenty, and to spare, for everybody; and that he should never have any harder work to do than running up to town with Mr. Black, and holding interviews with all sorts and conditions of men.

They saw printers and got estimates; they ticked off the best advertising media in " Mitchell's Newspaper Guide;" they looked at offices in the

City, they had long and confidential discourses with auctioneers and house-agents; they drove to Stangate and went over the mills, which were in full work, and in and out of which went and came men covered with flour, and of a generally white and dusty appearance; they dined at Wandsworth with Mr. Bailey Crossenham, and at Sydenham with Mr. Robert Crossenham.

They netted their thousands and their tens of thousands easily enough, after the ladies left the room, over wine which could not have been better. Capital, the Messrs. Crossenham agreed, was all that any business needed to ensure success. They made fortunes by the aid of pen and ink. Hundreds of tons of wheat — millions upon millions of loaves; the merest gains, the slightest margin of profit, swelled up to something almost incredible per annum. The Messrs. Crossenham were in the highest spirits about the new undertaking; but then certainly one fact concerning those worthy brothers must be borne in mind, namely, that they had been tottering on the very verge of bankruptcy when Mr. Black rushed to the rescue. This, which of course remained a secret amongst the trio, accounted for much that even in those early days puzzled Arthur Dudley—as, for instance, the intense respect wherewith these apparently well-to-do men treated Mr. Peter Black; the deference they paid to his opinions; the readiness with which they fell into all his views; the rapidity with which they seized and acted on his suggestions. There was not that independence cf manner about the brothers which Arthur considered their means and position might have warranted them in assuming; but the conclusion he drew from all this was that, clever as he thought Mr. Black to be, people who ought to know much more about the promoter than it was possible for him to do, thought him cleverer still; and, had anything been wanting to increase Squire Dudley's confidence in his leader, the manner in which that individual was treated by those with whom they came into actual contact, must have raised Mr. Black considerably in his kinsman's esteem.

To the men amongst whom they mixed freely, the promoter, in fact, stood precisely in the same enviable position as that dog who has got a good bone, down to other curs.

With a certain envious deference they followed

him, hoping to get a portion of the spoil, or the reversion, perhaps, of the bone itself, should Mr. Black by any accident drop it; whilst as for Arthur, the promoter had told and hinted such falsehoods concerning his position, his wealth, his tremendous pluck, his untiring energy, his determination to make the "Protector" a success, that the Squire was welcomed in the City with open arms, and became all of a sudden a person of consequence.

"Lord Kemms walks in and out of his house just as I might do in and out of yours," remarked Mr. Black, with calm impertinence, to a man who, though worth a hundred thousand pounds, and the owner of a fine place twenty miles from town, had utterly failed in all his attempts to get grander people to dine with him than Miller, a tallow-chandler, who dropped his Hs, and then following the universal law of compensation picked them up, and stuck them in where they had no business to make their appearance; who was for ever inverting his personal pronouns, and vexing the soul of the rich man's daughter with reminiscences which, though possibly faithful, were by no means pleasant to hear related in the presence of a limp young curate the lady hoped to fascinate.

It would have amazed Arthur to know that any human being held him in high esteem, because a lord was, truly or untruly, reported to be running loose about his house; and it might have annoyed him still more to know that the cool insolence of Mr. Black's words brought the man who was worth a "plum" on to the direction, where certainly no politeness or entreaty on the part of the promoter could have compassed such an end.

Behind the scenes Squire Dudley was never, however, permitted to peep. He saw the play go on, and was fascinated by its variety, its excitement, its rapid dialogue, its sunshiny hopefulness. How it was really got up, he had not a suspicion. That it was all tinsel and paint, and hollowness and sham, he had not a ghost of an idea.

It made a good show, and promised fair to draw a full house. Was not that the only thing which concerned him? Mr. Black was of this opinion, at any rate, and took very good care he should see none of the dirty work in course of execution. The unpleasantnesses and difficulties, present and to come, were all kept studiously out of view. The king was never beheld without crown and sceptre; if the queen ate bread and honey, it was partaken of with locked doors, and in a decorous privacy.

No fairy met Arthur's view destitute of gauze; unadorned with spangles, rouge, and pearl powder. The back of the canvas had no existence for him. If disagreeable letters arrived, Mr. Black did not show them to his coadjutor, but stated generally these private epistles concerned his other ventures. If a man's consent were doubtful, the promoter saw him first alone. On insecure ground he knew better than to let Arthur step; and if the Squire returned to his country home, thinking the new company had hitherto not met with a check, who can feel surprised?

Whenever there was the faintest chance of a gale, his clever captain got him into the cabin, and kept him there till the storm had blown by, or the danger was over.

He saw the life and the fun of the voyage, but none of the peril; and so he went back to Berrie Down brighter and more cheerful than ever, and Heather seeing him happy could not brace up her courage for the explanation Miss Hope assured her was essential, if she would save herself and the children from beggary.

Perhaps the part of the business which Arthur enjoyed most was that of assisting to write the prospectus.

On that document, Mr. Black asserted, hung the fate of the " Protector Bread and Flour Company, Limited," and the mutual talents of Arthur Dudley and Peter Black, Esquires, were employed for one entire fortnight in writing, correcting, and revising the production which ultimately went forth to the world, like many another great and good work, anonymously.

" It may seem an easy thing to write a prospectus," remarked Mr. Black. " The fellows that do histories, and novels, and newspaper articles, I dare say imagine there can be no trouble about drawing up an attractive advertisement ; but let one of them try to do it—that is all I say. Why, a prospectus combines within itself every literary difficulty you could mention : it has to be got up to suit the tastes of all readers ; it must contain something to tickle the palate of each man and woman who looks at it. Who is to check history, and say whether it is right or wrong ? but any fool can check statistics. I had a hack once, who used to do some of this kind of work for me, and he said it was all very fine for Macaulay and Alison, who could write just what they liked, and were not compelled to stick to facts, which are such stubborn things there is sometimes no dressing them up attractively or even decently; but he declared there was a heap of dry bones flung to us, and we have to compose out of those promising materials brilliant pictures, exciting romances, perfect blue-books full of sound statistical information. And what he said was true. Our style must be at once brief and persuasive. We must be eloquent in order to draw shareholders, and yet mindful that each word costs money. We must say nothing we are not prepared to verify. We must be as well up in grammar as in the price of shares. We must not slander our neighbour, nor unduly exalt ourselves; and yet we are bound to show that, since the beginning of time, the heart of man never imagined, and the brain of man never conceived, such a project as that which we have the honour of submitting to the consideration of the intelligent and discriminating British public."

"You should write a pamphlet on the subject," suggested Arthur, laughing.

"I wish I could—I wish I dare. It would be a comfort and a satisfaction to me to tell that same enlightened British public what I think of its sense. Upon my honour, Dudley, the worse your company is, the easier it is to write a prospectus about it. If you only want to float a thing, not to carry it through, why, you can say whatever you please about the matter, and the more you say the better the shares sell."

"And why do you not put down whatever you please about the 'Protector'?" asked his companion.

"Just because it is *bona fide*—because I must stick to facts and figures—figures that will satisfy not country simpletons, and ambitious widows, and discontented governesses, but sound commercial men. It is a serious matter, my friend, and must be wisely concocted and wisely executed. That is why I put in merely a preliminary advertisement hitherto. I knew the *grand coup* would require both time and thought. We must have a little of the moral, the philanthropic, the hygienic, the scientific, the statistical, and the profitable; and we ought to put a Latin quotation at the top: it will look classical, and complimentary to the attainments of the people to whom it is addressed. Greek might be better, or Hebrew; but I suppose you do not understand Hebrew?"

To which accusation Arthur pleading guilty, Mr. Black urged upon him the immediate necessity of "rubbing up" his Latin, and finding an appropriate heading for the prospectus.

"We shall want one to go round the stamp also," proceeded the promoter; "but that is not immediately required. Yes, it is, though," he added, "for I must mention the stamp at the end of the prospectus. Now, Dudley, look alive; if I do the composing, the compiling, and the inventing, surely I may depend on you for the Latin and correct English!"

After fourteen years, the Squire's classical education had the dust thus brushed off it, in order to furnish a plausible swindler with a couple of Latin mottoes.

For twice seven years he had kept this thing by him, that it might serve Mr. Black's turn at last.

"Dudley's!" said that individual, in frank explanation to his City friends. "Devilish neat and taking, ain't it? Bring in the parsons; they'll think the whole thing has been drawn up by some Oxford man, as the Latin was, for that matter, out of a well which has not had any water pumped from it for Heaven knows how long. If you have any suggestion to make on the subject make it, or else hereafter hold your tongues, for I am going to have the prospectus printed off to-morrow."

"Could not be better!" answered his friends in chorus; and the programme of the "Protector Bread and Flour Company, Limited," was accordingly sent down to Harp Lane, where it was printed (on credit) by a protégé of Mr. Black's, on a very superior satin paper, procured on credit likewise.

Next day after delivery, proof was duly forwarded, and the day afterwards the prospectus was returned —pressed, folded, multiplied a thousand-fold—to Peter Black, Esq., at the Temporary Offices of the Company, 220, Dowgate Hill. The bundle, containing programmes of the "Protector Bread and Flour Company, Limited," was flung down on the counter in the outer office of 220, Dowgate Hill, at five to five precisely, and, at three minutes to six, four hundred and twenty-five prospectuses were wrapped up, directed, stamped, and posted at the chief office, Lombard Street.

"She's off the stocks at last, thank God!" said Mr. Black to Squire Dudley, who stood beside him; "she's off the stocks and afloat!"

CHAPTER II.

MRS. PIGGOTT'S ASSISTANT.

IT was late on in the autumn by this time, and most of the visitors who had come down to the Hollow in the bright summer weather were now elsewhere.

Miss Hope, having patched up a peace with her nephew, was at Copt Hall; Mrs. Ormson at Torquay, with her eldest son, the state of whose health was considered unsatisfactory; Mrs. Black, at Hastings; Mr. Black, much in town; Mr. Harcourt, in Scotland; and Bessie, at home, keeping house for her father.

There was no one left at Berrie Down, in fact, excepting Master Marsden, who remained on at the Hollow, because the state of Dr. Marsden's finances prevented the boy being sent to school; while the state of his mother's health rendered it an act of real charity to keep the "noisy, ill-mannered, ill-conditioned young whelp" (this was Arthur's summary of him) away from that small, uncomfortable, wretchedly-managed suburban house.

Early in November, Alick was to enter on his new duties; and at Christmas, by special desire of Arthur, there was to be another and larger family gathering in Berrie Down. All kinds of people were to meet all other kinds of people; and the Hollow, he said, "should see Christmas kept in thorough good old English style, for once."

Already the younger Dudleys were speculating as to whether there would be an abundance of berries on the holly bushes, and Mrs. Piggott was looking to the fattening of her turkeys, and meditatively calculating how many of those unfortunate birds the expected guests would, in all probability, consume.

Already she was pouring into the ears of her youthful handmaiden, Prissy Dobbin by name, tales which sounded to that unsophisticated damsel like romances, anent the number of plums she should have to stone, currants to wash and dry and pick, about the quantity of mixed peel she must cut up, and the amount of suet she would have to chop, for the Christmas puddings. As for mincemeat, Mrs. Piggott avowed her intention of commencing that whenever the twenty-first of November was come and past; and had the Israelites been journeying, for a second time, out of Egypt, and purposed making a halt at Derric Down on their way, the worthy housekeeper could scarcely have "salted down" a larger quantity of butter, nor looked more anxiously at the tenants of the poultry-yard and the contents of the nests than she did.

As for herbs—Miss Priscilla Dobbin's private opinion was, that "the deuce was in Mrs. Piggott about them." For ever, so she told her mother, she was rubbing off those herbs into bottles, and tying them down; while, in respect of pickles, it is on record, the assistant made herself so frightfully ill with devouring those exhilarating articles of diet wholesale, that the cook assured her she should be sent home forthwith if she could not content herself for the future with cooler viands than chilies and chutnee.

"Drat them girls!" exclaimed Mrs. Piggott; "they're every one alike now—for crinolines, and vinegar, and piccalilly. I remember a young house-maid as used to come and see me when I was taking care of General Furdie's house in Gloucester Place

—I believe she used to live on pickles—bought them at the oilman's, sixpennyworth at a time, and if she came and sat with me for half an hour, she would finish the lot while she sat talking. Ah! girls ain't like what they used to be."

"And a good job too that they bain't," retorted Priscilla, who was certainly as unlike one of Mrs. Piggott's ideal maidens as can well be conceived.

Except that she could "get through her work," when she chose to devote herself to it, and that she was sufficiently "owdacious and comical" to make time pass fast in the Berrie Down kitchen, Priscilla Dobbin was not possessed, in Mrs. Piggott's eyes, of a solitary virtue.

She was not "one" the cook would ever have had about the house; but, of course, Mrs. Dudley knew best—a severely ironical expression, which meant that Mrs. Dudley knew nothing whatever about the matter; indeed, Mrs. Piggott had been heard to say, that "a baby in arms was as fit to choose a servant as her mistress."

After all, however, Priscilla was not exactly an importation of Mrs. Dudley's. A girl had been wanted, and this girl, a protégée of Bessie's, stepped

at once from a wretched home to service at Berrie
Down, where she worked harder, and idled more
persistently, than any young person " of her inches,"
that it had ever been Mrs. Piggott's misfortune previously to come into contact with.

And yet with all she was as good company, in
her rank, as Bessie Ormson in a higher; better,
perhaps, for she possessed artistic, histrionic, and
imitative powers, of which the young lady was
utterly destitute.

Miss Dobbin had been taught at school to curtsey,
or "bob," as she called it; but elsewhere she had
learned to dance with anybody, and to execute
"steps" which were the delight and envy of the
kitchen at Berrie Down. At school she had been
taught psalms and hymns and spiritual songs; but
out of hours she had acquired a stock of ballads that
would have horrified the propriety of the vicar of
North Kemms, Priscilla's native parish, had he been
privileged to hear them. At school she was taught
to read, write, cipher, and do sampler work; out of
school it had ever been her pleasure and delight to
mimic the peculiarities of mistress and master, of
clergyman and clergyman's wife, of the ladies who

visited the school, and of her fellow-companions, playmates, father, mother, and society generally.

She was but a young thing when she came to the Hollow, sixteen or thereabouts, with a scanty supply of clothes, a crinoline which was at once the plague and delight of her life, a net to contain her hair, and induce people to believe it was long like a grown-up woman's, and a stock of impudence that was, were Mrs. Piggott's testimony on the subject reliable, " more than enough."

With Priscilla it was not, however, perhaps, that she had so much impudence as that she had so little reverence ; and for this reason, spite of Mrs. Piggott's high social position, her imposing cap, her stately manner, and her reminiscences of the good old times, the young girl treated her with as little ceremony as she might one of her playmates, and "answered the housekeeper back,"—an indignity which had never previously been inflicted on that individual by anyone, gentle or simple.

" She had always lived with people above and below, as knew their places and kept to them, till ' you came,' " she stated to Miss Dobbin ; whereupon Miss Dobbin inquired—

"O Lor', there, ain't you glad I am come, that you may see some new life?"

Did Mrs. Piggott threaten to report Prissy to Mrs. Dudley, that young person entreated of her to make haste and do so, "before her shoes wore out." Did the housekeeper, talking at Priscilla, endeavour to point a moral and adorn a tale by stating what was done in her young days—and what her first mistress, the lady of Mr. Serjeant Hickley, counsellor to the King (so Mrs. Piggott understood K.C.), said when she saw a servant with a bow or a bonnet, let alone a flower, added Mrs. Piggott parenthetically—Priscilla, rich in ribbons, flowers, and laces, flung to her from Miss Ormson's stores, thanked her stars " she had not lived in them days, and thought it was quite time the good old times were gone and past, if anybody was to have any comfort of their lives."

" I'm sure I'm glad I warn't born then, Mrs. Piggott; for one thing I'd be as old as you, and have nothing before me; I'd have lived it all. and not have a thing to look forward to."

" Better have nothing to look forward to than some things to look back upon," answered Mrs. Piggott, sententiously ; which immediately elicited from Miss Dobbin the inquiry whether she had got that out of her own head or somebody else's, and if these were some things she did not care to look back upon.

Clearly, the housekeeper said the girl could come to no good, and yet in her heart Mrs. Piggott liked this feminine ne'er-do-weel, and would have felt the house lonely without her.

On the whole, she preferred Prissy's chatter to the more staid and sensible discourse of Jane, the housemaid, or Sarah, her assistant in dairy and kitchen. Though torture could not have wrung such a confession from her, Mrs. Piggott dearly loved gossip; and, if she had searched the home counties through, she could not have discovered a more industrious collector and retailer of news than Priscilla Dobbin.

From the colour of the moire antique the vicar's wife wore when she went to dine at Moorlands, to the name of Miss Amy Raidsford's " intended," Priscilla had every atom of parish information at her fingers' ends. Why the lady's-maid was dismissed from Moorlands—what Lord Kemms said when he found his gardener sending all the best fruit to Covent Garden, and only retaining windfalls for dessert at the Park—Prissy knew as well as though she had been present.

Nor was it only from the neighbourhood of North Kemms that Miss Dobbin collected materials for conversation. She knew all about the low marriage Mr. Harry Camperdon, the Fifield rector's son, had contracted with the sexton's daughter from Palinsbridge.

" And I wouldn't ha' married her if she had been hung with diamonds—should always ha' felt or thought she had been dug up out of the graves. Seen her?—to be sure I have, Mrs. Piggott—as thin as a hurdle, and as pale and sickly-looking as a bit of your underdone crust. She's a contrast to Mrs. Raidsford. You don't mean to say you have never had a sight of Mrs. Raidsford! then you have a treat to come; like the side of a house, and mean! would look after the candles' ends, if her husband let her, and grudges throwing away her nail-parings. There is not a servant in the house dare give a glass of beer unbeknown, and they all say a nicer gentleman nobody need wish to serve. It is thought Lord Kemms would make up to one of the daughters, if it wasn't for her; but he can't abide her. Well, if I was Lord Kemms, I know who I'd have—money or no money."

And so on, *ad libitum*, the whole day long. Making beds, cleaning plate, shelling peas, stirring preserves, Priscilla Dobbin's tongue never ceased; and let the burden of her song be what it would, the refrain never varied, and that refrain was to the effect, that, since time began, there never had been. before, and never would be again, such a young lady as Bessie Ormson. Bessie had made her acquaintance at a period of (to Miss Dobbin) infinite trouble. Having been despatched to the mill to purchase some flour, she contrived by the way to lose the money entrusted to her. Feeling it useless to proceed, and being afraid to return home, she did the only thing which seems natural to boys and girls under such circumstances, namely, lifted up her voice and wept.

While she sat on the stile leading away towards North Kemms, with her bonnet tilted over her face, her knuckles in her eyes, and making a display of feet encased in strong leather boots, and a pair of sturdy legs, which only the extremest distress could excuse being exhibited to public view, Bessie, coming along the field path, paused to inquire into the cause of such despair.

A greater contrast than that presented by the pair could scarcely have been imagined. Hot and weary with running about searching after the lost money, sick and tired with crying, and the fear of the "hiding," which she explained to Bessie was sure to follow on confession; her cheeks wet with tears, and her face generally smeared by reason of having been rubbed over with her dirty hands, Priscilla's personal appearance alone entitled her to the profoundest commiseration.

Attired, on the other hand, in the coolest of muslin dresses, with the most coquettish of hats for head-gear, with a lace shawl thrown carelessly round her, holding a parasol, edged with deep fringe, a little on one side, more apparently to protect the trimming of her hat than her bright, fresh, beautiful face from the rays of the sun, Bessie, leaning against the stile, held converse with Miss Dobbin concerning the loss she had experienced.

" It was a whole harf-a-crown, Miss," said the girl, amid a perfect gust of sobs, "and I put it in my pocket, and I never left the path the whole way, except to pull a branch of roses (the poor things were lying withered and miserable, sodden and faded in her lap), and I suppose it was when I reached up to get them the money jumped out; but I have looked and looked, and I can't see it. No, no more nor if it had had legs and run away. See, it was over in the corner of that far field. I'll show you, if you like," she added, with a faint hope, perhaps, that Bessie might be able to find where she had searched in vain.

"The scene of such a catastrophe has not the slightest interest for me," answered Bessie. "I will take your word that the half-crown is lost, and I will give you another in its place, or at least two shillings and sixpence, which comes to much the same thing. You go, or have gone, to school, I suppose?"

"Yes, Miss."

"Then you know what a moral means?"

"I think so, Miss."

"Well, the moral of this afternoon's work is: For the future, when your mother sends you out for flour, don't stop to gather roses by the way, for it is extremely unlikely that you will a second time meet any one in these fields worth half-a-crown."

Having finished which speech, Bessie, toying with her dainty parasol, still stood looking at the girl, for whom she felt that compassion, which always moved her when she saw anything of the feminine gender unkempt, forlorn, untidy, unhopeful, uglier than she had "a right to be."

To her, an ill-dressed girl or woman was precisely what a daub is to an artist, a series of discords to a musician. She loved prettiness. Let a woman's dress be of cotton or of velvet, she still loved to see that dress worn with a certain consciousness; and the terrible want of self-assertion, the utter abandonment of all self-appreciation in the girl who now stood opposite to her, was so distressing to Bessie, that she entreated of her as a parting favour to wash her face, and push her hair out of her eyes before she proceeded to the mill.

"There is plenty of water in the stream," Bessie added; "and do make use of it freely, for at present you look as if you had been buried without a coffin."

A week after, the young lady, who had forgotten all about this occurrence, was told that a girl wanted to speak to her—a girl from North Kemms—Priscilla Dobbin by name.

"She does not want another half-crown, I hope," laughed Bessie, when she heard the name; and she went out into the hall, looking, as she always did, pretty enough to drive any man to distraction.

"Well, Priscilla, you have not lost your money again, have you?" thus Bessie commenced the conversation.

"No, Miss—I found it. I could not rest; and so, the first afternoon mother could spare me, I had a good look, and I took one of my little brothers, and he got it in among a lot of weeds growing in the ditch; and here it is back again, please, Miss—and —my duty to you," finished Prissy, who evidently considered the last four words an appropriate ending to her sentence.

Bessie took the half-crown, and held it in the palm of her hand for a moment, doubtfully.

The coin had evidently been washed, as had also Miss Dobbin's face, which was painfully red and shiny. Then she looked at the thick clump boots, laced up with a leathern thong—at the sturdy legs, showing below the short, scanty, hailstorm-pattern cotton gown—at the little old-fashioned black pelerine—at the coarse school bonnet—at the light brown hair, cut so short all round—at the greenish-grey eyes, sparkling with pleasure—at the unmanageable mouth, which would smile and break into grins of delight at the recovery of so great a treasure—at the hard hands, that seemed to have done so much work—before she said—

"Sit down for a moment, I shall be back presently." She wanted to tell the story to Heather, and ask her advice; but, as Heather happened to be out of the way, Bessie returned to the hall discomforted.

She did not like to give the girl back the money, or its equivalent, and she was racking her brains what to offer, when Lally appeared on the scene of action, with a huge wedge of cake in her hand, which it is only right to state she was absolutely unable to eat.

"Lally, come here," exclaimed Bessie. "I wish to give this little girl something by which to remember me—something to remind her of having been very careless and very good. What do you think she would like best?" and Bessie took the child in her arms and waited, hoping, perhaps, the stranger might suggest some desirable memento for herself.

But Prissy never spoke, nor, for some time, did

Lally, who first stared at Priscilla from head to foot, and then gravely turned and looked at Bessie, wondering apparently whether that young lady could conveniently part with her face as an appropriate offering to the stranger.   Then her eyes wandered to Bessie's throat, and so fell on a tiny brooch which fastened her collar.   The moment they did so—

" Dive her 'at," said Lally, unhesitatingly, a suggestion which she would have made all the same had the trinket been worth a hundred guineas ; as it was, Bessie abode by her decision, and taking out the brooch, handed it to Priscilla, remarking at the same time that, " although she might not care for it then, she would perhaps when she grew up to be a woman."

Not to be outdone in generosity, Lally at once presented the girl with her piece of cake, assuring her it was " very dood," the truth of which statement Bessie doubted exceedingly.

Next day, over came Mrs. Dobbin to know whether it was " correct as a young lady at Berrie Down had given her gal a golden brooch ? She did not think her gal would tell a lie, but still young uns wanted to be looked arter."

Assured of the rectitude of the transaction, Mrs.

Dobbin, after having been refreshed with ale and a slice of bread and meat, was permitted to depart. "Altogether, the half-crown threatens to prove a costly matter," Bessie remarked; but Heather only said they seemed to be very honest, worthy people, and the subject dropped.

But when, a little later on in the summer, Mrs. Dudley perceived it would be necessary to procure some young person to assist in the housework, Bessie proposed that a trial should be given to Priscilla; and never ceased her entreaties for the girl to be engaged until Heather said Bessie and the girls might walk over to North Kemms and talk to Mrs. Dobbin about the matter.

Nothing loath was Mrs. Dobbin for Priscilla to " go out," " except," she said, " that in the matter of clothes she feared Prissy warn't fit to be seen in a gentleman's house."

" Let her come over to me, and we will arrange that," Miss Ormson answered; and accordingly, when Prissy came, out of her own wardrobe the young lady furnished that of the new servant— telling her at the same time, laughingly, she was " made up for life."

" And you may think yourself a lucky gal," re-marked the mother on the first Sunday when Priscilla went home, about a month after her entrance on her duties at Berrie Down—" having plenty of victuals, and good clothes to your back, and a kind mistress."

John Dobbin was sitting in the porch during this colloquy, looking askance at his daughter's finery the while. When she came to exhibit her new dress to him, he observed, first, that " fine feathers didn't make fine birds," and then inquired—

" Who was that chap I saw thee talking to last evening, this side Moorlands ?"

" I warn't out yesterday evening, father," answered the girl.

" Warn't thou ?"

" No," was the reply.

" Thou mayn't have told a lie about that harf-a-crown piece, but I doubt thou'rt telling a lie now, my lass," he said.

" Well, you can ask Mrs. Dudley if I went out yesterday," retorted Prissy, defiantly.

" I take it Madam Dudley has something else to do than watch the coming and going of a wench .ike thou," he answered ; " mayhap she don't know the one-half of what anybody in the house does; but I can tell thee this much, Prissy—that if I catches thee going wrong, I'll break every bone in thy body, if it was covered an inch thick with silks and satins."

"I warn't out," persisted Prissy.

"See that thou bain't then," returned her uncompromising parent; and as the weeks and the months passed by without John having any further occasion to find fault with his first-born, it may reasonably be presumed that she heeded his admonition.

Further, in a general way, she gave satisfaction at the Hollow, where she was on good terms with every one, unless, indeed, it might be Master Marsden, who was, as she took various opportunities of informing him, an "ill-behaved limb," and no "young gentleman."

The last occasion on which Priscilla found herself moved to this confession of faith, was when she boxed Master Marsden's ears for holding Muff, and instructing Leonard to rub turpentine over her coat, preliminary—so she ascertained from Lally, who came rushing to her in an agony of distress—to "making a bonfire of my poor tittens."

That Master Marsden never forgave this interference with his legitimate pleasures, and that his wrath was very grievously moved, both at Lally's tale-bearing and Prissy's prompt interference, may be gathered from the fact that he informed Lally she was a "nasty little tell-tale tit."

"Lally not," lamented the child.

"Yes, you are—and 'your tongue shall be slit, and every little puppy-dog shall get a little bit,'" persisted Master Marsden, with his own tongue very far out; adding, to Priscilla, by way of appendix to this poem—

"As for you, you ugly, snub-nosed, green-eyed little ——"

"No names, Harry," interposed Alick, who chanced to come up at the instant; "and what have you been doing with the cat? What's all this, I ask?" and he looked angrily round the group.

"I was only going to singe her hair; it is too long, like some people's tongues," answered the boy, impudently.

"Now look here, Harry," said Alick; "I won't take you to Arthur, because he would not lay a finger on you; but I'm your brother, and I'll give you a thrashing for this you'll perhaps remember. Teaching Leonard such tricks, too, you cruel little cur!"

"Cur yourself!" retorted Harry; and in a moment he was grappling with Alick, trying to wrest the riding-whip he held out of his hand—kicking, plunging, biting even; and all the time Alick kept shaking and striking him,—Lally crying bitterly the while—till, panting and frightened, the boy shrieked out for mercy.

Then the elder loosed his grasp and bade him go, saying, "Though you make such a noise I know you are not much hurt, but never let me catch you playing such tricks again, or I will hurt you next time."

"I'll be even with you all yet," observed Harry, gratefully, as he skulked away; and this threat, which probably had not the slightest meaning attached to it in the boy's mind, was remembered to his disadvantage subsequently.

When the day came that it was remembered, no one believed his declaration of not having "meant anything"—of not having intended to do anybody any harm. When every creature in the house treated him like a pariah, and avoided him as though he had leprosy, Harry felt that he could better have endured a dozen worse thrashings than such social ostracism. When his assertions were received with silent incredulity—when his questions were answered reluctantly and with withering disdain and dislike—when his food was handed to him as if he were some unclean animal, unfit to eat or associate with civilized beings—when there was a great silence in the house—when people went about on tiptoe, and, if they met the boy, passed him either with averted heads or with looks of reproach and anger—when Leonard turned king's evidence and bore testimony against him—when he sat in his own room, or else wandered about the farm, kicking twigs and stones listlessly before him—Harry felt it was all more than he could bear, and, turning at last on Cuthbert, told that youth he did not see why they were all so hard upon him. "You were not a bit better, any one of you, when you were young," he finished, passionately.

"*We* did not try to kill people," answered his step-brother, with dignity, as he retreated from the room, followed by Harry's indignant remonstrance of—

"No more didn't I—no more didn't I!"

CHAPTER III.

HEATHER'S DARLING.

IT was late in the autumn, as I have said ; the leaves were falling rapidly, and, but for the constant sweeping and supervision of "the boys," the walks and lawns at Berrie Down would have been littered with the decaying foliage.

As it was, barrowful after barrowful of dead leaves disappeared from the grass in front of the drawing-room windows, and often as not Lally sat on the top of the load which Alick or Cuthbert wheeled away to a corner of the kitchen-garden, and there deposited in a great heap to make leaf-mould for the next year's geraniums.

No more pride than Lally had these young Dudleys. If work were not to them prayer, it was, at all events, pleasure. It would have been a weary

E 2

life to those lads, lounging about the Hollow, taking purposeless walks, rising in the morning to do nothing, going to bed at night after having performed no task, executed no duty ; but, as matters stood, each season brought its labours with it to them.   They loved the place, and they loved Heather, and they loved work.

What need is there to say more ? because of all these reasons, Berrie Down looked the Berrie Down we have visited.

But a change was coming, and Heather knew it —knew Alick was going away, that her best helper was about to be taken from her.   Many a talk had the pair held together over the inevitable parting ; many a word had they exchanged in the twilight, under the shadow of those dear old trees ; and, if Alick thought Bessie's words and talk had been more sad and more attractive, still he knew Heather's discourse was the best, and so listened to it attentively.

" You have been my very right hand, Alick," she repeated over and over again ; " and I do not know what I shall do without you."

" Nor I without you, mother," he answered, sadly.

" And you are going all alone, my boy, to a place which every one says is very, very wicked. I do not know much about wickedness myself, Alick," she added, with that sweet simplicity that made her seem so inexpressibly innocent to people who *did* know much about that wicked world, which was a *terra incognita* to Heather Dudley ; " but I hope, dear, that a person may be as good in London as in the country ; that you will not be led away, nor fall into expensive habits, nor associate with undesirable people, if only for my sake, Alick."

" You darling mother !"

" If ever anyone asks you to do what is wrong, if you are ever tempted to extravagance, to folly, or to sin," she added, " think of me at Berrie Down, and of how your trouble would grieve me, Alick, will you ?"

" Mother, there is no need for fear ; I hope there is no need."

" I hope not, either," she answered ; " but yet who, setting out to travel a strange road, can tell what companions he may meet with by the way—what troubles may assail him ? More than all, Alick," and the sweet voice which was never hurried, never much excited, grew low and pleading as she spoke, "If ever you do fall into any trouble, promise to come and tell me; promise, whether I can help you or not, to come and talk it over. If you cannot come to me, I will go to you; and do not think any sin or sorrow—however bad it may seem to you—too bad to tell me. If you have to bear its consequences, I can bear to hear of it. Promise me, Alick! If I think you mean to keep no great sorrow from me, I can let you go—not otherwise."

"Mother—Heather—what are you afraid of?" he asked.

"I am afraid of nothing except the indefinite," she answered, through her tears. "It is a new country to me this life on which you are entering. Were I going to explore it myself, probably it would not seem so terrible. Promise, Alick."

"I promise," he answered; and then their talk flowed on to calmer ground—to such commonplace affairs as, "where he should lodge, what amount of worldly belongings he should take with him, what edibles it would be advisable for Heather to send for him to his London home."

In all these minor matters Mrs. Dudley was

intensely interested; not that the other subjects on which she had touched lay farther from her heart, but only that they seemed less within her province than such homely affairs as seeing that his linen was in proper order, that he had flannels for the winter, and an abundant supply of towels and soap; to say nothing of more animal luxuries, in the shape of fresh butter, preserves, poultry, and eggs.

It was arranged how all these necessaries, which Mrs. Piggott believed were to be had genuine nowhere out of Hertfordshire, could be forwarded periodically to London; and then Heather set to work on Alick's wardrobe—condemning socks, examining shirts, turning over collars, and so forth.

"Alick had better take everything new with him," she said to Agnes, "and leave these for Cuthbert;" and the poor soul sighed.

Perhaps she felt intuitively Alick would never require her again to furnish him with an outfit—that from the day his foot passed forth from Berrie Down he would never need hosen nor shirt from her more.

The great change was at hand, such as arrives to the mother when her darling marries a husband able to provide her with her heart's desire, and more than her heart's desire, if such a thing were possible; to the sister, whose brother's wife takes from that day forth to all eternity charge of the mending, airing and making of an idol's linen, and it was natural at such an hour Heather should desire "her boy's" wardrobe to be unexceptionable, that she should wish the very stitches in his collars, the very marking of his clothes, to remind him of the "far-away home," where she would never cease praying he might be kept from all the temptations of the world, the flesh, and the devil.

Dear Heather; oh! dear, dear Heather! I know cleverer women do greater things than your imagination ever compassed—that they write books and paint pictures, that they compose music and preach sermons, that they scribble reviews and manage warehouses, that they are owners of various business establishments in the City, and serve writs to unsuspecting debtors; and yet I doubt if all these mementoes of women's work and women's talents would rest so long in the mind as one sweet word from you!

All this time she had full leisure to devote to Alick, for Arthur was away, staying at no other place than Copt Hall, where, through the instrumentality of Miss Alithea Hope, both he and Heather had been invited to spend a week.

Of his cousin, Arthur had hitherto known as little as his cousin knew of him; but on her return to Copt Hall, after many years of absence, it became the desire of Miss Hope's life to promote an intimacy between the respective families.

"He is your own cousin," she said to Walter Hope, "and it is really scandalous that you do not visit each other;" acting on which hint, often repeated, Mrs. Walter Hope wrote a very gracious note to Heather, trusting she and her husband would spare them a few days before all the fine weather was gone. Mrs. Walter Hope laid considerable stress on the point, that she and Mr. Hope were much distressed at the fact of such near relations and neighbours remaining for so long a time comparative strangers. She hoped for the future they should see more of each other. She had heard so much about Mrs. Dudley from dear Miss Hope that she felt as if she (Heather) were quite an old acquaintance. She described the best railway route from Palinsbridge to Foldam (the station nearest to Copt Hall), just as if Arthur had never journeyed there in days gone by, and begged to know on which day and by what train Mr. and Mrs. Dudley were likely to arrive, in order that the carriage might meet them.

Never was a more cordial letter penned, and Arthur, with new prospects of wealth before him, did not read it ungraciously.

On the contrary, he extracted an augury of success from these overtures of friendship, and urged upon Heather the advisability of accepting Mrs. Hope's invitation.

But Heather did not wish to go, at least not at that particular juncture. She had much to do, she told Arthur. She had to set her household in order after the summer visiting; she had to make and to mend; she wanted to be with Alick during the latter part of his sojourn at Berrie Down; she was tired, really tired, of talking and company, and desired rest; all of which reasons only provoked Arthur, and caused him to declare that she thought of every person except him, and acceded to every person's wishes except his.

Then Heather, with a smile, told him she knew he was not in earnest, and added that she had another reason for wishing to remain at home, viz., the state of her wardrobe.

"Dress which is quite sufficient for me at Berrie Down," she said, "would scarcely be suitable at Copt Hall."

Upon that Arthur gave his wife a fifty-pound note, and bade her get what she wanted; but Heather, turning very white, folded up the note, and handed it back to him, saying, "I would rather not, dear; I would, indeed——"

"And why not?" he demanded.

"Because I do not think we can afford it," she answered, "at least not yet," she added, seeing how vexed he looked.

"Not yet! Will you tell me what you mean, Heather?"

"Why, I mean, Arthur, that though you have not told me anything of what you are doing, still, I cannot be blind. I see the stock gone, the crops sold. I know you are engaged in some business with Mr. Black, and that there is money needed for it. You would never have sold the crops so soon, had there not been a necessity for selling them; and then, Arthur, perhaps, when Christmas comes, you may want all the money we can save, and I should not like to spend any unnecessarily now."

"I shall have money long before Christmas," he answered.

"You may," she said, "but you may not. I cannot tell what it is you are doing or expecting, but——"

"Hang it!" broke in Arthur, "is a man bound to tell his wife everything? When you can't help me—when you would only be trying to dissuade me from my purpose, and keep me from ever rising out of the slough of poverty in which I have passed year after year—why should I talk to you about what I am doing or expecting? Women's ideas are so contracted; they take such short views; they are so cautious, and so fearful, and so fond of certainties, that there is no use in even trying to make confidantes of them. Because you are happy yourself here, Heather, you think I ought to be so too ; because you can endure the cursed monotony of such a life, you would keep me bound to the wheel for ever."

"I think you are a little mistaken," she answered. "I have been very happy here; I do love Berrie

Down very much; but I would leave it to-morrow, and go with you anywhere in the world, if I thought by so doing I could contribute to your comfort, happiness, or prosperity."

"If you thought," he repeated. "Ay, there's just the rub; you never could think so."

"If *you* thought that leaving Berrie Down would make you happier, I would do it. I would do anything for you. I have tried to please you, Arthur," she went on, speaking almost entreatingly. "I have never contradicted your will. I have never put myself in opposition to you. I have never teazed you with questions. I have striven to do my best; but, as you are not satisfied, tell me how I can do better; and it shall not be my fault if I fail. Only, Arthur, only don't let us drift away from one another; don't let us begin to have secrets, and treat me as though I had done something to shake your trust and confidence in me."

Never before had Arthur Dudley seen his wife so moved; never before had he heard such a sentence from her lips. For a moment he felt tempted to tell her all; to make a full and ample confession; to explain to her not merely that his stock was gone, and his crops also, but that he had put his "name" on paper, to an extent which, if the Protector Bread and Flour Company failed to fulfil the hopes of its promoters, would certainly cripple his resources seriously.

Of course his name was only "lent;" but occasionally misgivings would cross his mind that in the event of any hitch occurring, he might be liable for the whole amount of every bill which was at that moment wandering about London, passing from hand to hand.

If the Protector "smashed up," to use Mr. Black's concise phrase, Arthur Dudley would be smashed up with it; he had gone on little by little, till he was afraid of reckoning how much of Berrie Down was set up in type at Printing House Square, and in various newspapers throughout the country.

If the Protector failed—but then the Protector could not fail—and because it could not fail, and because if it did fail, so much must go with it, Arthur decided not to tell his wife (who would be certain to look on the worst side of things), but to humour her, as Mr. Black recommended, and answer—

"I do not know, Heather, what you mean by drifting away; you and the children are never out of my thoughts by day or night. I have gone into a very good thing with Mr. Black, in company with Lord Kemms, Mr. Allan Stewart, Mr. Aymescourt Croft, and a number of other persons, all gentlemen of position and fortune, not likely to rush into any foolish speculation. I hope to be a wealthy man yet. I hope to get rid of this eternal worry about money—which makes life not worth the having. I know you would help me, Heather, if you could; there, there, don't look pitiful. I can't bear it. There is nothing you can do for me now, except buy yourself some handsome dresses, and come over to Copt Hall."

She put her hand out to take the money, then a second time she returned it to him, saying, "Let me have my own way this time, Arthur; when you have made your fortune, I will spend as much money as you like; only till you have made it, I should not feel happy to be extravagant. Don't be angry, love!" she pleaded; "don't be vexed because I ask to have my own will for once in a way."

"Once in a way!" repeated Arthur. "Always,

you mean, don't you ? No, I'm not angry ; stay at home, if you like. I do not think that there are many husbands who would press their wives so much to accompany them ;" and with this undeniably true remark, Arthur Dudley strode out of the room, leaving Heather to think over the matter at her leisure.

Very patiently she did so—very resolutely she took up the facts of her married life, and looked at them from beginning to end. There was nothing new in what she saw—nothing. It had been coming upon her for months past, that she did not possess— had never possessed—her husband's love. When she beheld Gilbert Harcourt's devotion to Bessie, she knew Arthur had never been similarly devoted to her. She was not the love of his life, and neither was she the friend of his heart. He trusted in others ; he confided in others. What was the reason of all this ? Was it a fault in herself, she wondered. If it were, how did it happen that the boys and the girls, the men-servants and the maid-servants, and the stranger who came within their gates, all turned to her for sympathy and companionship ? Without any undue vanity, it was still impossible for Heather not to know that she was greatly beloved by those with whom she came in contact; and yet, what was the use of being beloved, if the one person on earth she cared for threw her off?

Threw her off! Had they ever been near enough for him to do so; were not they quite as near now as ever they had been? Was it not only the blessed darkness of her mental vision which had hitherto kept her from discovering this fact? "He never loved me," Heather decided—"never; and he has found it out too late."

And then there came over her soul a terrible pity for him, which swallowed up all sense of personal wrong—all anger—all selfishness. She could not unmarry him; she could not give him the woman he might have loved, the wealth that might have made him contented. She was no heroine—this Heather of mine; tragedy was not in her nature. The idea of freeing him from the yoke under which he had voluntarily put his neck, never occurred to her. To flee to the ends of the earth, to part from him, leaving a note of insufficient explanation behind; to rush off with the first man who whispered a few civil words to her, and let her husband walk through the Divorce Court to liberty; to purchase a little bottle of poison and kill first her children and then herself—these very feasible and proper courses, were ideas which never even crossed Mrs. Dudley's mind.

Outside of lunatic asylums, amongst the decorous and unexcitable people to be met with in society, or when we take our walks abroad, we are told, by those who profess to know their fellow-creatures thoroughly, that such impulsive, devoted, unselfish creatures exist; but Heather's imagination never soared to such heights of passionate self-sacrifice.

They were married, and the time for even thinking of parting with Arthur being past for ever, all she could do was to try to make him as happy as possible.

For who could tell? like David, she thought that the Lord might yet be gracious to her, that some day, perhaps, Arthur would know how much she loved him, and give her back a portion of love in return.

But, meantime, she never blinded herself—from the hour knowledge began to dawn, she never refused to open her eyes and see the dull grey morning-sky of reality which had broken for her. Though she did not sit down and weep, still she made no attempt to fly from the presence of her trouble. There came no change over her face, unless it might be that the lookof which I have previously spoken, oftener sat like a brooding shadow across her eyes. She did not weary her husband with her affection, or load him with caresses; yet, although an ordinary observer could have detected no difference in her manner, Arthur had long felt there was a change; that his comfort was more considered, if that were possible, than formerly; that his every wish was anticipated; that his caprices were more attended to, his com-plainings more rarely combated, than of old. He felt there was a change, though he could not have put a name on that change; and as it irritates sick people to be humoured, so it irritated Arthur to find that even the faint opposition of old was withdrawn —that, let his commands be as unreasonable, as fretful, as provoking as they would, they were still obeyed implicitly.

Never, excepting where some question of right and wrong was involved, did Heather lift up her voice in opposition to his, and he was, therefore, the more annoyed and surprised when Heather ventured to demur about going to Copt Hall.

"So deucedly provoking, too, when I wanted her, and just at this time," he remarked to Mr. Black, whom he met in London—that being the route he took to Copt Hall — whereupon Mr. Black said, consolingly—

"That, perhaps, it was as well ; Mrs. Dudley might have put her foot in it."

"She would have come if I had pressed her, you . know," continued Arthur, not wishing Mr. Black to believe Heather the better horse at Berrie Down ; "but I was not going to do that."

"You had a bit of a tiff, I suppose, is about the English of the matter," commented Mr. Black. "Well, such things will happen, even in the best-regulated families."

"We had no tiff," answered Arthur ; "my wife is the last woman on earth to make a row about anything."

"I am aware of that, of course," said Mr. Black, drily ; "but still she does not go to Copt Hall."

"Oh ! damn Copt Hall !" exclaimed Arthur.

"No, no, don't do that yet—not, at any rate, till

we see if Walter Hope, Esquire, J.P., will appear on our direction—eh!" suggested the promoter, poking Arthur in the ribs, and winking slyly as he spoke. "Never mind the wife, Dudley, she'll come to, no fear, when she sees our spec succeed, and you keeping your carriage and horses, and having your box at the Opera, and God knows what besides. Don't trouble yourself about any persons' thoughts now; their thoughts will be all right when you have a clear five thousand a year, and the chance of adding another five to that. Never fear; those that win, laugh, you know."

And with this assurance Arthur departed for Copt Hall, where he was most cordially received and most hospitably entertained, and where he met again, after years, Mr. and Mrs. Douglas Aymescourt Croft.

Meanwhile, Heather remained at home, doubtful whether she had done right in refusing to accompany her husband, in throwing cold water on his proposal that she should array herself like the Queen of Sheba, and thus attired, repair to the courts of Arthur's relatives.

She could not decide the question to her own

contentment—she could not satisfy her understanding as to whether, when a woman promises to obey a man, she thereby excludes herself ever after from all title to take up her own parable and express her opinions boldly.

She knew other women had no such qualms of conscience—that to most of the wives she knew obedience was a dead letter; but this did not prevent Heather fretting and fidgeting. She had vexed her husband at a time when she wanted most to please him, and he had told her before he left, when he saw her busy with preparations for his brother's departure, that she "liked Alick better than she did him—that she thought of studying every person's pleasure sooner than his."

"I do not know what to do, I am sure," she reflected, as she drove over to South Kemms in an old tumble-down, rattling phaeton, that was the very shame of Arthur's life, but which she, nevertheless, preferred to the, in her opinion, still more dilapidated fly from the Green Man at Fifield, which was in the habit of conveying visitors to Palinsbridge Station; "I do not know what to do." She had written every day to Arthur since his departure, but never a line did he vouchsafe to her in return, and she was wondering whether she ought or ought not to write again.

"Of course, if I do not teaze him to answer, if I merely send a line to say we are all well, it cannot seem like worrying," she decided; and having so decided, she made her purchases (which were principally in Alick's interest) at South Kemms, returning home with Ned, who was charioteer, as the evening shadows were settling down upon the Hollow.

When she reached the door, Alick was there to help her alight, and carry in her shawls, and wraps, and parcels.

She was full of her little purchases : a woman must, indeed, be in a terrible state of despair—a depth of despondency too great for a spectator to contemplate calmly—when the prospect of opening a draper's parcel fails to send a thrill of expectant pleasure through her heart.

"Take them into the dining-room, Alick," she said. "Oh! I am very glad to see that fire, it is so cold out of doors ;" and she walked into the apartment and pulled off her bonnet and threw back her mantle, and stood with her hands stretched out towards the blazing coals, warming her numbed fingers.

"Where are the girls?" she asked, at length.

"Upstairs," Alick answered, stooping over the parcels he had brought in as he spoke.

"Is anything the matter?" Heather asked, quickly turning from the fire. He had only uttered one word, and yet his tone filled her with a vague alarm.

"Is anything the matter?" she repeated, finding he did not reply. "Alick, look at me; why do you keep your face turned away?"

Then Alick looked up, but his eyes fell under Heather's scrutiny.

"Alick, tell me this instant what is the matter," she said. In a moment her fancy conjured up all sorts of horrors—her husband was dead, there had been a railway collision, perhaps. Thought is sometimes as quick in our waking moments as in our dreams; and her imagination flew to him over all the miles that intervened between them. "You have heard bad news," she went on. "Is it about Arthur; is he ill?"

"Not that I know of," Alick answered. "But, mother, we have had an accident since you went away."

"An accident!" she repeated. "What kind of an accident—what is it—who is it? Alick, you will drive me mad if you stand there looking at me without speaking."

He tried to speak, but he could not do it; he had been nerving himself up to tell her, and now, when the moment came for explanation, the words died away upon his lips.

"Heather," he began, in a tone of deprecating entreaty,—and then suddenly the truth flashed upon her.

"It's Lally," she cried; "it's Lally; oh! my child."

He caught her as she was about to rush past him out of the room. "Mother, mother," he said, "listen to me; she fell into the mill-pond, and they brought her home, and the doctor is here, and we have been doing everything."

"And she is dead!" finished Heather.

"No, she is not," said Agnes, entering at the moment. "She has this instant opened her eyes;" and she broke out sobbing almost hysterically.

"Thank God!" exclaimed Alick, solemnly, after the manner of a person rescued from some fearful danger.

Then Heather, looking from one to the other, understood that while she had been driving to South Kemms, and making her purchases, and never thinking of evil, her darling had been standing in the very valley of the shadow—that she had brushed garments with the angel of Death; and her first feeling, when she did understand all this, was, not one of gratitude that her child was saved, but of anger and resentment at her ever having been permitted to get into danger.

She had not encountered the ordeal which the younger Dudleys passed through while Lally lay seemingly dead before them; she had not fought for the child as they did, both before and after the doctor's arrival; she had not endured the agony—an agony not to be described—which filled Alick's heart when he met the little body being carried home across the fields; she had not ridden for the doctor and followed him from house to house as hard as the best horse in Arthur's stables could gallop; she had not stood in suspense by the bedside; she had not wondered with them, "How shall we tell Heather—what will Heather say?"

That had been the one thought of every person in and about the house,—"What will Heather do; what will Mrs. Dudley say!"

The very regret for Lally seemed merged in dread of her mother's sufferings.

How should any one face Heather and tell her Lally's life was still problematical? Who should prove brave enough to break the tidings to her, and look upon her agony?

Through the whole of this suspense and anxiety the younger Dudleys had passed; but how was Heather to understand everything in a moment? The only certainty she comprehended was that her darling had been left to get into danger—that she had almost lost her child; and so she cried aloud in her terror and her anger,—

"Was there not one of you that could have seen to her—not one amongst you all?"

They never answered her — they could not tell her then how it had come to pass; they were so thankful at even a chance of life being given to the child, that they did not mind the mother's reproaches, though it seemed strange to them to see Heather angry.

There are times when it appears a less weighty trouble to behold a friend angry than sorry; and so they bore her blame in silence, and made way for her to pass out, only remarking—

"She is very ill, remember; had you not almost better stay downstairs for a little time longer?"

As if she did not hear their words, Heather walked blindly across the hall, groping her way to the staircase. When Alick would have taken her by the arm, she thrust his proffered help aside, and guiding herself by the balusters managed somehow to reach the first floor.

There she paused, and put her hand to her head, seemingly trying to remember something.

"She is in your room," Alick said, thinking she wished to know where the child lay; but it was not that; as she tried to move forward again, she tottered, and, had Alick not caught her, would have fallen.

"Lay her on my bed," Agnes whispered; and Alick accordingly carried his burden into one of the pleasant chambers, the windows of which, however, now looked forth on lifeless trees and bare brown branches, waving mournfully to and fro in the night, as the autumn wind rushed across the deserted fields and over the Hollow.

CHAPTER IV.

POOR LALLY.

TIME and tide, we are assured, wait for no man; which, though a truth, is but a portion of one, since happy would we be if, in this world, time and tide were the only things that refused to delay their departure for our convenience.

There are many circumstances of our daily lives against which it would be as vain to appeal—to which it would serve quite as good a purpose to cry aloud for mercy, as the typical hour and tide.

For the first time in his life, Alick Dudley realised this fact, when he found he must depart for London, and leave Heather in the very midst of her trouble, with no one at hand to "see after her," so the lad expressed himself.

"I will," said Agnes, reassuringly.

" Yes ; but you are not a man, Aggy," he answered ; "that is the worst of it." And though, in some respects, Agnes was almost as good as a man, still she sighed deeply, feeling her inferiority.

What was there a man could not do? A man could lift heavy weights, and think nothing about them ; a man could fling a saddle on a horse, and put a bridle in his mouth, and gallop off for a doctor, without first going about the house wondering whom he could send ; a man could jump into the mill-pond and bring Lally out, holding her suspended in mid-air, as a cat does its kitten ; a man could go out in all weathers, he could undertake to break bad news ; the very sound of his voice in the house was a reassurance ; his very tone of command a trumpet which recalled the scattered senses of a tribe of frightened females. Without Alick—boy though he almost was—what would Berrie Down be ? a camp without a chief. Even if Arthur were back, they would all miss Alick. He was so prompt, he was so daring, he was so utterly unfeminine in every respect.

Now, many feminine qualities were possessed by Arthur ; and, therefore, even if the Squire had been at home, he could never have proved of the same use in the house as his much younger brother Alick.

There has been a great deal written of late years about masculine women. It seems rather one-sided for no one to preach against feminine men; for if a woman be objectionable in so far as she resemble a man, a man must surely be objectionable in so far as he is dependent, and weak, and timid, and faint-hearted, and undecided, and variable, and impulsive, and easily influenced, and speedily depressed, and equally speedily rejoiced, and governed by the opinions of others, and dependent on external influences, like a woman.

I lift my hand in supplications, and cry earnestly for mercy, ladies, as I finish this sentence, which I believe to be true as sorrow and pain. There is another cry which is popular now-a-days, and the man or the woman who raises an opposition shout is likely to find small favour in the crowd; but the opposition shout is none the worse for that.

A man is a divine institution, even in a domestic point of view. He may not be charming pottering about a house, counting the camellias, and instituting inquiries into the items of a grocer's bill ; but he is at a premium when a gun wants cleaning, or a troublesome tramp grows insolent.

In precise proportion as he fails to load his pistols, or face a danger, whether moral or physical, as he is lazy, self-indulgent, wanting in energy, his merits fall below par; and the man, spite of his sex, in point of usefulness is at a discount.

Never at a discount Alick Dudley was likely to be; and that truth, even while she sighed, Agnes dimly grasped. She did not know, she really could not imagine, what they were all to do without her brother ; more especially at that juncture, when there was terrible sickness in the house — when, more than ever before in her life, Heather wanted help, and consolation, and encouragement. And yet Alick must go ; the laws of the Medes and Persians were as likely to be reversed as the rules hung up in the clerks' office in the great warehouse of Messrs. Elser, Wire, Hook, and Elser, Wood Street, City.

Time and tide would about as probably wait the convenience of mankind, or humour the whims of womankind, as those gentlemen accept as apology for Alick's non-appearance the fact of his niece being ill, and his sister-in-law in trouble.

According to the mood in which the firm chanced to be, the members composing it would have intimated to Alick, either that it was a matter of the supremest indifference to them if the whole of his relations were dead and buried, or suggested that he had made a mistake in applying to them for a situation, since it was evidently a nurse's berth he wanted at one of the hospitals.

But, in whatever form of words they had couched their rejection, that rejection would have certainly been inevitable. No blame to the Messrs. Elser and Co. Of course the world cannot stand still because children fall ill, and women like to have their male relations near them in times of trouble.

Heather, indeed, would have been the first to recognise this truth, had there arisen any question concerning it ; but in that quiet Hertfordshire home it never occurred to a single soul within its walls that there could be a moment's hesitation in the matter.

Alick had to go ; and, accordingly, he packed up his clothes, bade good-bye to "the mother," not without tears, kissed all his sisters, received quite a volume of maternal advice from Mrs. Piggott, together with a box of sandwiches, prepared, apparently, under an impression that he was going to the Canary Isles, and had not the remotest chance of getting anything to eat till he arrived there; and, in the grey dawn, drove over in the pony cart to Palinsbridge, where he caught the eight o'clock up-express, and entered the office of Messrs. Elser, Wire, Hook, and Elser, at ten—the hour at which he had been bidden to put in his first appearance.

On the same day two letters were posted at Fifield: one to Arthur from Agnes—written in defiance of Heather's wishes—telling the Squire of Lally's accident, not lightly, as Heather had done, but fully and circumstantially, and informing him how ill, how very ill the child had remained ever since; and another, which having been penned with a great expenditure both of thought and ink, it may be as well to print it *in extenso*, for the information of my readers:

At " bury-donne yollow

"fiefield

" arforshyre,"

it purported to be written, and the date was Monday, —— 18—:—

"dere mis"—it began—"this coms with my dewtey hopeing yu ayre in good helth az it leves mee at preasant.

"dere mis, i hope yu will pardon the libberty i tayke in riting, but az wee are all in grate distres i thought praphs az yu mite like toe no.

"it's along of mis laly, who was nere drownded last Weak and who as layd almost for Ded yver since. dere mis it was al along of mastar marresden Which is az yu no a very bade Buoy, tha was al down at the mil, and miss laly She were a-standin cloze up to the brinck, wich were rong in she, but the Pore darelying new no Beter, when mastar marresden he sais to mastar lenarde—goe and giv her A Pusche and soe he Pusched hur inn, and she Was for Yver and Yver soe long in the Watter for the tew others was soe frytenned thay colde doe nothyng but schream, and at Laste the myler's yf—She herde the crise and mr. scrotor he Mayde noe more addoo than intoe the Watter after hur, and Shee has bene verry bade yver sinc and Pore mrs. duddeley is like wun broaken Harted. She Wente of wen shee yerd the Knus, and it was a Long time befor shee comed too agen. mis laly is rowled up in franell and cryse a gode diel and dere mis i doant no wot is the mater with shee, but I Am Afraide it is hur death. mrs. duddeley she sais her Pore chylde is beter too-nite but i think it is Only a temporeairy feling. mrs. pigot sais shee thinks mrs. duddeley would be beter if her concert wuz at whome, but mrs. duddeley woan't hav him rote for, were i think she is rong. but dere mis i rite to yu without askhing noboddy's lefe, and i hop as you will Xuse the libberty. i have knot seen yu no whu sinc yu Went—and ples mis knot to sai az i have rote, becaus mrs. duddeley mite think az i had took to Mutch on mee, but i beleav yu augt to noe, and so hopeaing i have don rite i remain dere miss, with dewty,

" Yur yver afeckshionate thoe umble

" serveant

"prishila dobin."

Without photographing the original document, which cost Miss Dobbin quite as much mental anxiety as an official dispatch, it would be vain to hope to give an idea of the sort of manuscript through which Bessie Ormson at length arrived at the fact of Lally's serious illness.

It was blotted all over by accident and design. If by chance Priscilla spelt a word rightly, so surely she rubbed her finger through it, and wrote in another as unlike what it ought to have been as can well be imagined.

She had not a capital letter in its proper place from first to last, and it was many a day, in fact, before Bessie fully mastered the contents of that epistle.

But she gathered enough, almost in a first perusal, to convince her something was very wrong at the Hollow; and, although she had no invitation from Heather to do so, still she instantly resolved to start for Berrie Down.

With Bessie, as a rule, to resolve was to perform; and, accordingly, that very same evening, she astonished the Dudley household by walking coolly in amongst her cousins as they were sitting down to tea.

" Well, and what is this about Lally ? " she asked, after she had kissed the girls, and inquired for Heather ; " what is the matter with her ? "

" Did Alick not tell you ?" answered the assembled Dudleys in chorus.

"Alick," repeated Miss Ormson. "I have not seen Alick. I only heard a vague rumour this morning about something wonderful having occurred, and so I thought that I would come down and learn the certainties of the matter for myself. One of you girls, I think, might have written to tell me; but I suppose it is with you as with the rest of the world—out of sight, out of mind."

"Heather would not let us write to any one," said Agnes.

"Then Heather ought not to have had her own way," retorted Bessie; "and then, I suppose, she has been up with that child night after night, taking no rest, eating nothing, fretting herself to death."

"We all wanted to sit up," exclaimed Lucy Dudley, "but she would trust no person."

"Precisely what I expected," said Bessie, who had by this time divested herself of cloak and bonnet, and now stood beside the fire looking as trim and pretty as though she had just stepped out of her dressing-room. "And so Lally is very bad?"

"That is precisely what she says herself," answered Laura. "Whenever the pain leaves her for a minute or two, she settles down a little in the bed and whispers, 'Poor Lally's very bad.'"

"Is she in danger?" asked Bessie.

"I do not know; the doctor will not tell us."

"Is Arthur at home?"

"No; Heather would not let him know how ill Lally was," answered Agnes; "but I wrote yesterday —not that I suppose he could do any good, if he were here."

"She fell into the mill-pond?"—this was interrogative.

"She was pushed in," answered Cuthbert, with a vicious look towards Harry, who sat at the farthest corner of the table with his legs tucked up under his chair, a great slice of bread and butter and honey in one hand, and a huge cup of tea in the other.

"I didn't push her in," remarked that young gentleman.

"No, but you told Leonard to shove her," said Cuthbert, shaking his hand at his brother menacingly.

"Well, how was I to know she would topple over like that?" persisted Harry. "If she was loose on her perch, that wasn't my fault, was it? and it's not right of you to go on like that at me. Mrs. Dudley said you wasn't to do it; she came and she talked to me, she did, and said she believed me, if nobody else didn't."

"She must have great faith," remarked Bessie, meditatively. "If I had been here, Harry, I should have taken you down to the pond and given you a ducking on my own responsibility."

"I shouldn't have cared if you had drowned me, then," retorted Harry. "There was not one of them would speak to me, and Alick would not let even Leonard come and say a word to me; and I was so miserable, I often thought of going out at night and throwing myself into the water, and that I knew would vex them all—only I was afraid of crossing the fields by myself in the dark;" and at the bare recollection of his fear and trouble, Harry began to whimper.

"If you had done that, you know," said Bessie, coolly, "you would have been buried at the four cross-roads on the way to South Kemms, with a stake through your body."

"I should not have minded what was done to me when once I was dead," said Harry, philosophically.

"If you do not mind what you are about while

you are living," answered Bessie, "you will come to the gallows."

"No more likely to come to the gallows than you, Miss Impudence, for all your red-and-white face and shiny hair, that you think so much of ;" and Harry put out his tongue as far as he could thrust it at Bessie, who, without "more ado," to appropriate an expression from Priscilla's letter, walked round the table, and would have boxed the offender's ears but that he disappeared from his chair and dived among the feet of the four Dudleys, one of whom, Cuthbert, was not slow about availing himself of the tempting opportunity thus offered.

"You're a coward," said the boy, reappearing on the other side with a very red face, and his hair all in a tangle, looking, as Laura said, like one of those things chimneys are swept with. "You're a coward, to kick a man when he's down. Come on, and fight it out."

"You had better behave yourself, Harry," answered Cuthbert, "or I will give you toko for yam," which mysterious threat evidently conveyed some definite idea to Master Marsden's mind, for he answered :—

"You could not, nor two like you."

"Shall I try?" asked Cuthbert, rising; but Harry fled towards the door, and Agnes ended the quarrel by bringing the boy back to the table and seating him in his place, and warning both him and Cuthbert that they must not make a noise—that the doctor had said the house was to be kept as still and quiet as possible. "So, Harry," continued his sister, "do be good for once in your life; finish your tea and go to bed."

"Yes, that's the way," grumbled Harry, his mouth full of bread, and his lips smeary and sticky with honey — "that's the way; finish, and go to bed; finish, and go into the garden; finish, and see what the men are doing; it is always go, go, go, from morning till night."

"Will you be quiet, and let other people hear themselves talking?" said Bessie, sharply.

"There are not many that would care to hear you talk, at any rate," retorted Master Marsden; "it is gab—gab—gab; bub—a bub—a bub—wherever you are, just like a meat-fly, or a wasp, or a mosquito."

"I declare, Harry, I will write to your papa," averred Bessie, solemnly.

"Write—who cares—and send somebody to read it, will you? We always call yours fat writing at home, and pa says if there was many hands like it, ink could not be made fast enough to supply people. Writing, do you call it? I could write as well with a paste-brush."

"Are you going to be quiet, Harry, or are you not?" asked Bessie, taking a step towards him; "for, if you make another saucy speech, I will box your ears, as sure as my name is Bessie Ormson."

"Who gave you that name?" mocked the boy; whereupon Bessie proved as good as her word, and, seizing him, was about to administer condign punishment, when Harry cried out—

"If you do—if you do—I'll make a noise, and then Mrs. Dudley will come down to know what is the matter, and then I'll tell her, and then she'll be angry with you, for she said nobody was to speak crossly to me while I stayed in the house."

"It is quite true," Agnes said, in answer to Bessie's look of inquiry. "She thought we were not kind to him, and scolded him about Lally; and in the middle of all her own trouble, of course, she had time to consider Harry. You see the result."

"And pray, Harry, how long are you going to stay in the house?" inquired Bessie.

"As long as I like—as long as I find it convenient," replied the boy; "but now, I tell you what; I am quiet mostly, not because I care a button for all their threats, but because I promised Mrs. Dudley I would—there now!"

"You are a curiosity," remarked Bessie.

"Not so much of one as you are. I don't wear frizzle-gigs of things in my hair; I don't live in a steel cage; I don't screw myself in round the waist and walk this way," added Master Marsden, marching up and down the room in a style which he firmly believed to be an exact imitation of Bessie. "I don't look from under my parasol—so! and make up my face when anybody is in the room I want to think well of me; I don't wear kicking straps and dress improvers to make my petticoats stick out—like that;" and Master Marsden pulled out his knickerbockers to their fullest width, and treated society to another representation of Bessie "sailing across a room."

If every one belonging to her had been dying at that moment, Bessie could not have refrained from laughing; and in this mirth her cousins joined.

"I suppose Harry thinks that is holding the mirror up to nature," said Lucy Dudley, at length.

"No, Harry does not," retorted the young gentleman; "he thinks it is holding the mirror up to art."

"I am art, then, am I?" inquired Bessie; and Harry nodded assent.

"Well," she said, "since it seems you have engaged this room for your performances, I will go upstairs and see Heather."

"Had not I better go up first, and tell her?" suggested Agnes.

"Oh no," answered Bessie; "good wine, you know, needs no bush;" and with that she left the apartment, and ascended to the sick chamber, at the threshold of which she paused for a moment irresolute.

The door stood wide open, and across the entrance was hung a curtain, so that the watchers could pass in and out noiselessly.

Lightly Bessie lifted this curtain, and looked in. On the bed lay Lally, quiet enough to have satisfied all Mrs. Ormson's requirements—quiet enough and changed enough—a mere shadow of the Lally Bessie had scolded and teazed, and loved and petted in the glorious summer weather—a poor wasted little Lally—a Lally who was, as she herself said, "very bad indeed."

And beside the bed sat Heather, looking so pale and worn that it might well have been supposed she also had passed through very grievous sickness. The blue-veined lids were closed over the weary, aching eyes, when Bessie first lifted the curtain; but she had scarcely time to glance at the child and her mother, before Heather, feeling there was some one standing in the doorway, awoke and recognised her visitor with a start of glad surprise.

Making a sign for Bessie not to make a noise, she rose and came across the room.

"I only heard this morning," the girl whispered, "and I could not rest. How is she?"

"Better, I trust," Heather answered. They were by this time in Bessie's old apartment, which looked as though she had only left it about an hour previously. That was the beauty of the Hollow—any one could drop into his accustomed place there, even after long absence, in five minutes.

" Heather dear, you have suffered dreadfully."

" Yes; but God has been very merciful," Mrs. Dudley answered. "Oh! Bessie, if she had died without my seeing her, I could not have borne it; there is no use in saying I could, for my heart must have broken. She has been frightfully ill. She was so long in the water, and then lying in her wet clothes while they carried her here. It was this side of the pond, you know, Bessie; and though Mr. Scrotter's house might have been nearer, still it could not have made much difference in her recovery, and it has made all the difference to me having her at home. Fortunately, there were good fires in the house, and plenty of hot water. If there had been any longer delay, we cannot tell how it might have turned out. The girls and Mrs. Piggott, Doctor Williams says, really saved her life; but I do not know—it seems to me everybody did what was possible. The worst of it was her being so long in the water, and so warm when she fell in—they had been racing, it appears; but if we can get her over this—and, please God, she will get over it—Doctor Williams assures me there is no reason why she should not be as strong as ever."

"I have come down to help you nurse her," said Bessie. "Now, don't begin making objections, Heather, because I know every sentence you would speak, and all I intend to reply is, that I mean to do my share of the watching, or else let Agnes take it in turns with you, and I will try and see to things about the house—only I am resolved you shall not kill yourself. What will Arthur say when he comes home, and sees you looking like a ghost? I declare, if I met you in the dark you would frighten me. Now, you shall lie down on the sofa to-night, and I will sit beside Lally."

"But you will be completely knocked up."

"You do not know much about my constitution, evidently," answered Bessie, smiling: and thus the difficult matter was arranged, and thus once again Bessie Ormson became an inmate of the Hollow, where Arthur arrived on the following day, greatly to Heather's vexation; for she had tried to keep this trouble from him, not wishing, poor soul, to "spoil his holiday."

But Agnes' letter was so imperative, that the moment he read it he packed his portmanteau, asked his cousin to let him have the dog-cart as far as Foldam Station, and travelled by various circuitous routes from that out-of-the-world-place to Hertford, where he thanked Heaven when he exchanged the Eastern Counties line of rail for the Great Northern.

"That Copt Hall is the most cursed place in England to get either to or from," he remarked to Bessie.

"I have heard some ignorant people remark that Berrie Down Hollow is not the most accessible spot on earth; and I know I thought it rather out of the way the other evening," answered Miss Ormson.

"It is next door to everywhere in comparison to Copt Hall," he replied.—"So you really think," he went on to say, "there is no fear for Lally now— little monkey! Heather looks bad, though, does not she? I declare, Bessie, it was very kind indeed of you to come down, and I am greatly obliged to you for it."

"Thank you, Arthur," answered Bessie, demurely; "it is a happiness to know that my poor endeavours to give satisfaction have found favour in your eyes." But although Miss Ormson replied to his gracious speech with so little appearance of astonishment, still she was secretly greatly surprised at the increased urbanity of his manners. "Arthur is growing like other people," she said to Agnes Dudley. "Saul is coming among the Prophets. I wonder if the Protector Bread Company have had any share in effecting this great change; if so, success to it, say I; may its career be happy and glorious—may its dividends prove satisfactory, and my uncle grow more prosperous, and more like a Puffin than ever!" And then she returned to her watch beside Lally, who crept out of absolute danger, surely though slowly, and at length grew strong enough to sit up in bed, supported by pillows, and toss over scraps of coloured ribbons and bits of silk that Bessie would spread out over the coverlet for her.

After a minute or two, however, she would get weary of this game; the red and the blue would begin to dazzle her eyes; the little hands would grow too weak to toy among the bright trifles; the head would get tired with trying to raise itself over the edge of the sheet; and when all these things came to pass, Lally would drop the latest scrap of silk—heave a heavy sigh—look piteously at Bessie, and declare "Lally's very bad aden."

"No, you are not," Bessie invariably answered; "you are scheming—you like being in bed this cold weather, and having nice things to eat, and being made much of; but wait a little. Some fine morning I will rout you up, and chase you about the lawn, and run you to earth in the Hollow. Won't I; do you think I won't?" and the lovely face was laid on the pillow beside the child, and Lally made nests for herself in Bessie's hair, and was fain to fall asleep holding on by her pretty nurse's gown, or sleeve, or collar.

"Oh Lor', Miss, ain't she like wax-work!" remarked Priscilla Dobbin, the first time she beheld Lally sitting up on Miss Ormson's lap—held in Miss Ormson's arms.

"She is much more like bone-work to my mind," answered Bessie, kissing the little white arms; "but we are going to feed her up, and send her to market next time her papa goes to London—are not we, Lally?"

And Lally, complaisant as ever, answered, while busily engaged in counting over the buttons on Bessie's dress, "Iss."

CHAPTER V.

MR. BLACK'S TARTAR.

PETER BLACK, ESQUIRE, of Stanley Crescent, sat in the Secretary's room at the temporary offices of the Protector Bread and Flour Company, Limited, 220, Dowgate Hill, looking as much like a thrashed hound as it was possible for so pompous, and prosperous, and self-sufficient a gentleman to look.

As a rule, wherever he went, and with whatsoever manner of person he came in contact, Mr. Black comported himself as if, so Mr. Ormson familiarly said, "he was cock of the walk;" but now Mr. Black had met with a bigger and stronger, and more arrogant cock than himself; a bird whose beak was strong and spurs sharp—who was accustomed to lording it over creatures of his own species —who would have been immensely astonished had

Mr. Black flown at him, and disputed his supremacy; but who, had such an affront been offered, would soon have cowed and discomforted his adversary.

Mr. Black, however, mindful perhaps of his victories on other fields, was content to rest on his laurels, and refrained from striving to wrest any from the crown that bound in City circles the brow of Allan Stewart, Esquire, of Walsey Manor, Layford; Careyby Castle, Perthshire; Hyde Park Gardens, London; and 92, King's Arms Yard, Moorgate Street.

With a man who gave himself airs, Mr. Black might perhaps have tried to get the mastery with success.   He might have deferred, and flattered, and listened with apparent earnestness, while all the time he was winding his opponent round his finger; but Mr. Stewart gave himself no airs; he did not aw— aw like the half-pay majors and poor middle-aged, dilapidated, disreputable swells with whom Mr. Black had so often come in contact. He did not quote Latin, and talk of his great friends, like the patientless doctors and surgeons, and the parishless parsons and the clientless lawyers, who also had been unto Mr. Black's eyes familiar as the breath of life in his nostrils.

He was not recklessly indifferent to results, shamelessly greedy concerning money, openly careless as to whether a scheme floated or not, so long as he got out safe and netted a few hundreds, after the fashion of the insolvent esquires and bankrupt merchants, who would not—so Mr. Stewart declared —have scrupled to put their names on the direction of a railway to the infernal regions, if only such statistics with regard to fares had been procurable as would have enabled them to show shareholders a prospect of a large dividend.

"They would glibly tell the British public what Charon clears per annum, and state that great inconvenience was felt by passengers when the Styx was rough and the winds contrary. They would sell their names to anything on the earth, or in the waters under the earth; in land, or sea, or sky; in this world or the next, if only promoters' and directors' fees were to be had out of the scheme. Those are the kind of men you have been accustomed to deal with, Mr. Black. It may save us, therefore, a vast amount of trouble hereafter if you clearly understand now that I am a different sort of man altogether."

Mr. Black inclined his head, and observed, somewhat confusedly, that he did not doubt it in the least.

"Excuse me," said Mr. Stewart, "but you did doubt it. You thought when you paid me that money, and promised me so many shares, and I gave you leave to use my name, and said I should go into the thing with you, that there was an end of me. You thought, when you heard I was abroad in the autumn, and at Walsey since my return, that I meant to leave the company in your hands, and meddle no further in the matter; but, pray, do not think so any longer. I intend to take an active part in this business. I mean that it shall succeed; and I have not the slightest scruple in informing you that it shall not be made a refuge for the destitute by anybody."

"I am at a loss to follow your meaning, Mr. Stewart," said Mr. Black, in answer.

"I will try to explain myself more clearly," went on the great man. "When you came to me, and I said I could not entertain your proposal without a retainer, do you know what my object was? No! Well, then, I took your five hundred pounds as a guarantee for your honesty. The sum was nothing to me; but I had no intention of having my time taken up about a company, the shares in which might never be worth *that!*" and Mr. Stewart snapped his fingers contemptuously. " I am perfectly plain, you see. I knew you had been connected with company after company. I knew, in fact, you were by profession a promoter of very bad schemes; but I knew, also, you had plenty of push, and that, if you saw it was worth your while to make a company succeed, you stood a fair chance of forcing it to do so."

Mr. Black bowed. These were the first civil words Mr. Stewart had addressed to him during the interview; and, although the amount of compliment they contained might not be excessive, still there was a certain recognition of his executive and imaginative talents conveyed in them.

For which reason Mr. Black bowed.

" Now, if the thing be to succeed, it must not be swamped with sinecures and a multitude of ground landlords."

Well enough Mr. Black knew all Mr. Stewart implied by that sentence; but, nevertheless, he asked him for further information.

" By ground landlords, I understand a number of persons who, considering the newly-discovered land their own, want to make off it as much as they can before anybody else touches a farthing—for instance, you are a ground landlord. Quite as well as I you know that Crossenhams' mills are not worth the name of the price you have put upon them."

" I assure you it is the very lowest price the Messrs. Crossenham would take."

" And that lowest price you share with them. I am not quarrelling with such an arrangement. The prospectus could not have been put forth without some mills being secured—and, perhaps, those mills are as good for the purpose of advertising from as any other; but still I happen to know all the ins and outs of that transaction,—that your paper has been keeping Crossenham afloat, that the machinery is very old, that the buildings are very dilapidated, and that, in fact, if you had not rushed to the rescue, Messrs. Bailey and Robert Crossenham must have been gazetted ere this, and that, in the event of such a calamity happening to them, the premises could have been bought for an old song."

" What has that to do with me?" asked Mr. Black. " A man must live; and, like you, I cannot afford to spend all my time, and strength, and thought, and money, only to receive payment in shares."

" True," said Mr. Stewart, with a dubious smile, which, however, encouraged the promoter to remark further—

" The labourer is worthy of his hire."

" Humph! that depends," observed Mr. Stewart.

" On what?" asked Mr. Black.

" On how much work the labourer does, and on the extent of his hire."

" Oh!" murmured the promoter.

" Your hire has not been excessive, as hire goes," went on Mr. Stewart, " *so far;* but I think you have run about the length of your just tether. I suppose, Mr. Black, you are now satisfied, and mean for the future to rest content, with your extremely moderate supply of paid-up shares?"

" Did you think I was going to *give* the public this company?" demanded the promoter.

" If I had ever entertained such an idea—which

I never did—you would speedily have disabused me of it," answered Mr. Stewart; "but the point on which I now desire information is this: Are you going to be content with your promoter's fees, with your shares, with your profits on the Stangate mills, with your commission on printing, advertising, travelling, and the Lord knows what besides, or are you not?"

"I desire to make no further claim," answered Mr. Black.

"Then what is the English of this item—' Lease of premises in Lincoln's Inn Fields?'" demanded Mr. Stewart, referring to a paper in his hand. "What the devil do you mean by even proposing that the offices of the company should be stuck up there? We shall next be paying for the goodwills of depôts in Highbury New Park and Camden Square."

"I do not see why the offices should not be in Lincoln's Inn Fields," observed Mr. Black.

"And I do not see why they should be in any such graveyard," answered Mr. Stewart. "Deuce a thing there is in Lincoln's Inn except lawyers' offices, and one or two places where they insure lives, and preserve skeletons, and grant licences to kill. What connection has Lincoln's Inn with bread-making?

I must bring this matter before the board, but thought, in the first instance, I would give you a chance of explaining yourself to me."

Mr. Black looked at the speaker, and turned the last clause of his sentence over before replying. Meanwhile, Mr. Stewart stood on the hearth-rug, with his coat-tails tucked up over his arms, airing himself in true British fashion in front of the fire. In this attitude he looked a man of whom no person would have cared to solicit a cheque—to whom no defaulting debtor would have cared to prefer a petition for time in which to pay.

A gentlemanly-looking individual, no doubt, who could have handed Lady Grace down to dinner in an aristocratic and suitable manner — who could have received one of the blood royal after the fashion which is popularly supposed to obtain at Court ceremonials; a very charming personage, doubtless, when complimenting young ladies on their singing, or asking materfamilias if all those velvet-tuniced lads were hers; but not a nice man with whom to discuss money matters, not a pleasant man to try to take in—to strive to wind round your finger—to endeavour to make use of.

Vaguely, Mr. Black, looking up at his grey-haired, hard-featured, plain-spoken visitor, grasped all this ere he answered :

" Lincoln's Inn Fields is as good a place as any other in which to have our permanent offices. The address reads well. It implies to the country imaginative lawyers; and lawyers, it pleases country people to think, know what they are about. Further, it is central. Gentlemen will not get their broughams knocked to pieces coming there, as they would do if they ventured with West End coachmen into the city. Moreover, if strangers staying at an hotel ask for Lincoln's Inn Fields, any idiot of a waiter can direct them to the place. There is something about the sound of Lincoln's Inn Fields which recommends' itself to me. I cannot think why you object to the situation, Mr. Stewart."

" I object," answered Mr. Stewart, " on two grounds: first, that I consider Lincoln's Inn Fields an unsuitable position ; and secondly, that I consider the whole affair a job."

" A job !" repeated Mr. Black, reddening.

" Yes, sir, a job," was the reply. " Who is this Mr. Dudley ? How does he chance to be the owner of that desirable leasehold property which you are trying to get the company to buy? I see his name on the direction. Who is he?—what is he? Is there such a person as Arthur Dudley, Esquire? Is there such a place as Berrie Down Hollow at all?"

"What have I done, Mr. Stewart, to justify such suspicion?" the promoter virtuously demanded. "Have I tried to deceive you; have I made any false representations; did I enlist you in our ranks by any undue means? If you are not satisfied with the company and with me, why not resign; why not disassociate yourself from us *in toto?*"

Mr. Stewart laughed. "How long would your company live without me?" he asked: "how long would your other directors remain on the board, if I withdrew my name from it? Rather, Mr. Black, I might say, if you do not relish my interference, why do you not resign, why do you not take your shares and your promoter's fees, and your various little perquisites, and devote yourself to those other companies which have very decidedly been neglected while you were employed in dry-nursing the Protector Bread and Flour Company, Limited?"

" That, then, is what you want me to do?" said Mr. Black.

" No; I only, following your lead, suggested a course which I thought you might find it advisable to pursue. I mean to interfere in this company. I mean that it shall pay, and I do not mean that it shall expend enormous sums on the purchase of freehold, copyhold, or leasehold property, when renting offices and shops will serve our purpose equally well, or better. That house in Lincoln's Inn Fields shall not be bought—at that point I take my stand. The proposal is ridiculous; the situation is undesirable; the price asked preposterous. Mr. Dudley seems not to be overwhelmed with modesty, or he never would have even thought of mentioning such a sum."

" He knows nothing on earth of the value of pro_ perty," Mr. Black declared.

" Oh, then it is your price. I thought as much; and you are to share the profit with him?"

" No," the promoter eagerly replied; glad, at last, perhaps, to find some point where he could contradict Mr. Stewart with advantage. " No, Mr. Dudley is the person who found the capital to work this company. So far, he has not derived one shilling benefit from it. He is not a business man; he has gone into this scheme solely on my recommendation."

" Is he an idiot?" asked Mr. Stewart.

" I have not associated much with idiots," was the reply, " and am therefore less competent to decide that question than you might be. But I should say, no. Considering he is a gentleman, and apt to believe what people tell him, I never saw any especial weakness of intellect about him. He is not rich, and yet he has, as I said, found the money to carry this matter through. When those premises in Lincoln's Inn were for sale, I advised him to buy them, and promised that they should be purchased by the company at a considerable advance on the price he paid. I consider the sum asked a fair sum; whether he make a profit or not, is no concern of ours."

" Of mine, you mean," amended Mr. Stewart. " It may be very much of your concern."

" I am not to have a penny piece out of the transaction, if that be what you would imply," Mr. Black replied.

" That was what I intended to imply," said the other; " and if it be a fair question, Mr. Black, how did you chance to meet with this *rara avis*, who found the money to 'start your company and believed all you told him ?"

Many a time in his life Mr. Black had been bullied, and rebuffed, and snubbed, and irritated, but never before, never, had he been so coolly insulted—so insolently addressed, as by the very ordinary-looking, elderly individual, who, still airing himself at the fire, looked the promoter over—turned him inside out, as calmly as though Mr. Black had been a bale of inferior goods submitted to his inspection.

There was an offensive superiority in Mr. Stewart's manner which was very gall and wormwood to the person he addressed. Mr. Black would have liked to order him out of the office, and to have enforced that order with a due administration of boot leather; but, recollecting that kicking Mr. Stewart out would not help him personally along the road to fortune, he wisely restrained his feelings, and answered—

" I do not consider your question a fair one at all, sir. I never before came in contact with a gentleman who would not have hesitated about inquiring into such private particulars; but I have no objection to telling you how Mr. Dudley and I became acquainted. My wife is his aunt by marriage; that is how I came to know anything of Squire Dudley, of Berrie Down."

"Now what the deuce does that mean?" said Mr. Stewart, reflectively; "aunt by marriage. You are not Mr. Dudley's uncle, I presume?"

"Certainly not."

"Then is Mrs. Black's sister Mrs. Dudley?"

"She was until after her husband's death, when she married a second time. There were four sisters," glibly proceeded Mr. Black, "all daughters of Alderman Cuthbert; one died young, unmarried."

"The gods loved her, then, we may conclude," said Mr. Stewart, grimly.

"The eldest daughter married Mr. Ormson, of Cushion Court, with whose name, I dare say, you are well acquainted."

"Yes, as that of a very honest, respectable man," acquiesced Mr. Stewart, in a tone which implied that he never expected to hear one-half so much good of the person he addressed.

"The second did me the honour of linking her fortunes with mine," went on Mr. Black, at which speech his auditor smiled again, not pleasantly. "The youngest married Major Dudley, of Berrie Down, and——"

"Is, consequently, this Squire Dudley's mother," suggested Mr. Stewart.

"No, his mother-in-law," amended the promoter.

"Stepmother, you would say, I presume," corrected Mr. Stewart. "So that is the relationship, is it?" and apparently he constructed a genealogical tree for his own edification on the instant, where hung prominently a matrimonial excrescence, with a pretty face and vulgar manners, sister-in-law to Peter Black, Esquire, of Stanley Crescent.

"Major Dudley's first wife, the present Squire Dudley's mother, was a daughter of Arthur Hope, Esquire, of Copt Hall, Essex."

"Indeed!"

"You may have observed Mr. Walter Hope's name on our direction?"

"I believe I did notice it."

"You can make what inquiries you please about

Squire Dudley," went on Mr. Black; "indeed, the more inquiries you make, the better I shall be pleased. His position is perfectly unimpeachable. Excepting that he has not so much money as his friends could wish, I am not aware that there is a fault to be found with him or his surroundings."

"For a man short of money, the purchase of a house in Lincoln's Inn Fields was surely a venture," remarked Mr. Stewart.

"He bought it, as I have said, on my advice," answered Mr. Black, who could be brave on occasion; brave as well as self-asserting. "I thought, considering that with me originated the idea of this company; with me rested its very existence; on me devolved the organizing, carrying out, and perfecting of this scheme; I thought, I say, considering all these things, that when the concern came to be floated, a few of my suggestions would be received, and that I might do, at once, a good stroke of business for the company with which I was connected, and for the man who had stood by me and backed me up through thick and thin."

"Your imagination outran your discretion, then," remarked Mr. Stewart. "It is a dangerous thing for a man to try to benefit other people. Observe, the financial field has been reaped almost bare before he thinks of his acquaintances. You reaped and gleaned, Mr. Black, and then you wanted a second crop for your friend. We allow your claims, but the claims of your acquaintances and relations must go to the wall."

"I will give up three hundred of my claim on the mills, Mr. Stewart, if you do not oppose the purchase of those premises in Lincoln's Inn Fields," said the promoter, earnestly.

"Then the affair is serious?" suggested Mr. Stewart.

"It is very serious," answered Mr. Black. "Here is a man with property, worth, at the outside, ten thousand pounds, shall we say, and he advances money for advertising, and backs us up in every possible way with money, influence, connections. As a douceur for that, I advise him to buy that damned place in Lincoln's Inn Fields, fully intending that he should receive a good price for it from our company ; and now you come, Mr. Stewart, and put your foot in it ; you come interfering, and meddling, and——"

" Mr. Black, do you know how many shares I hold in this company ?" asked Mr. Stewart.

" A couple of hundred," was the reply.

" Exactly two thousand," answered Mr. Stewart, " and I mean them to repay me. They will not do so, as I said before, if we commence by making this company a refuge for the destitute ; and although, no doubt, your friend Dudley is a delightful fellow and a confounded fool, still, with him I take my stand. Those premises may be rented if you will, but never purchased. Please to remember what I say, Mr. Black—never purchased."

Utterly crestfallen the promoter looked—utterly like a thrashed hound or a disappointed pick-pocket. Stronger and stronger grew the inclination to kick Mr. Stewart off the premises ; feebler and feebler grew his hopes of controlling the operations of the Protector Bread Company, Limited ; and through all there was an awful sense of injustice—of it being a sin for him not to be able to do what he liked with " his own ;" with the baby he had conceived and brought into the world, and nursed into a great prosperous creature, the shares in which were already being eagerly inquired for.

" Then, what is Dudley to do ?" he asked, feebly and impotently.

" Sell the place again as soon as possible," advised Mr. Stewart.

" That is all very well ; but if he cannot sell ?"

" In that case he must let."

" And if he do not let ?"

" In that case he must make the best he can of a bad bargain,"—and Mr. Stewart shrugged his shoulders, as much as to say, " If a man will be a simpleton, he must bear the consequences."

" The matter shall come before the board," remarked Mr. Black.

" There is nothing to prevent its doing so, is there ?" inquired Mr. Stewart.

" And I wish to Heaven, sir—I wish to Heaven—I had been content to abide by good advice, and never asked you for your name, or influence, or—or anything," finished Mr. Black, in a fine frenzy. " I could have carried the company through without your help ; I should have been better without your interference ; I should have had the management, to a certain extent, in my own power, instead——"

" Instead of having some one on the direction

with an interest in the well-being of the concern," finished Mr. Stewart, who had by this time changed his position, and stood with one arm resting on the chimney-piece, staring into the fire. " Look here, sir," he went on, suddenly altering the tone in which he had hitherto spoken, " it is as much your interest as mine that this company shall succeed. It may make a rich man of you if it do—it will certainly ease me of a considerable sum of money if it do not. Our hopes, therefore, are, or should be, identical. Is it to be peace or war between us? Will you work with me, or will you work against me? Are you going to make posts and give salaries to all the men you ever knew since you started in business? Do you mean to show Squire This and Captain That where a good stroke of business is to be done—where a snug nest-egg is to be obtained? Are you going to advance the well-being of the company, or make it subservient to the well-being of Jack, Tom, and Harry? How is this to be, sir?—let us clearly understand one another at once."

" Is all this tirade merely because I advised Squire Dudley to purchase that house in Lincoln's Inn Fields?" asked Mr. Black, sneeringly.

" No, sir; all this tirade, as you are pleased to call it, originates not at the doings in Lincoln's Inn, but at the various other doings in Dowgate Hill. Here, for example, who the deuce is this fellow Harcourt, solicitor ? Nobody knows who he may be, except that he is some friend or relative of yours. Then, again, there is Bayley Crossenham, Esquire, manager; Robert Crossenham, Esquire, secretary *pro tem*. It shall not be *pro tem*. long, believe me. Then the bankers are your own; the auditors are the same whose names were appended to that most rotten scheme of yours, the City and Suburban Gas Company; the brokers are men of comparatively no standing whatever; not a soul on the direction but has been " qualified " by the gift of paid-up shares. I do not quarrel with that latter arrangement, for, with one exception, I think you have, so far as I can see, got a list of very good names—names that, perhaps, were worth paying for.   By-the-way, I perceive Lord Kemms is on the Direction."

" Yes," replied Mr. Black, wincing, however, a little at the implied question ; " he is next neighbour almost to Squire Dudley."

" Indeed, what a delightful person this Squire

Dudley must be! And so, because Lord Kemms chances to be near neighbour to Squire Dudley, he allows his name to grace our prospectus? I should not have thought it."

" Why should you not?" asked Mr. Black, sullenly.

" Well, for one reason, because he has been at Vienna for the last four months."

"I saw him, at any rate, in Squire Dudley's house, when I was down in Hertfordshire last summer," answered Mr. Black.

" And he gave you permission to use his name?"

" Certainly. Do you think I should put it on the direction if he had not?" asked Mr. Black.

" Have you any letter from him to that effect— any written authority to do so?"

" Even in the City we think a man's word sufficient authority," was the reply. " I do not know what code of honour may be observed among your relations, Mr. Stewart."

" It is best not to depend too much on honour," answered that gentleman, coolly. " If Lord Kemms took it into his head, on his return home, to re- pudiate the transaction, do you know what would be the result ?"

"Our company would probably find itself in Queer Street," replied Mr. Black; "but I am not afraid of that. Lord Kemms is not a man to back out of a promise, particularly if it can be made worth his while to keep it," added the promoter, *sotto voce.*

"I did not quite catch the last portion of your sentence," remarked Mr. Stewart.

"It was of no consequence—merely a passing reflection," said Mr. Black. "I can show you Mr. Hope's authority, and that of your nephew, Mr. Croft, if the sight would afford you any gratification."

"Thank you—they are of no consequence," was the reply. "I should have liked to see Lord Kemms', because, from 'information I have received,' I did not think his lordship would join us."

"He would not have joined us had Mr. Raidsford's persuasion carried much weight."

"Indeed! Who is Mr. Raidsford—his confessor?"

"Come, come, Mr. Stewart, do you think I am quite a simpleton?" demanded Mr. Black. "Do you imagine that piece of acting can take me in? I know who has been setting you against me—

I know who has been putting you up to ask if the names are genuine—if permission to use them have really been given. You have not so long left Mr. Raidsford's office as to have forgotten who and what he is; and I know who and what he is—a sneak and a toady, who has worked himself up from nothing with a smooth tongue and a spying nature. It was through tale-bearing he got on—perhaps it will be through tale-bearing he may get down."

" He is rich, then ?"—this was interrogative.

" Mr. Stewart," said the promoter, desperately, "don't you know all about Compton Raidsford, as well as I know about you? Don't you know he is very rich—so rich that he would not touch shares in the Bank of England? Don't you know he hates all companies—that having grubbed his own way up, he believes anybody else can grub up unassisted also? Don't you know he is a prying, meddling, conceited, cursed upstart?" finished Mr. Black.

" I cannot say that I do—in fact, I cannot say that I know the man at all," answered Mr. Stewart.

" Well, you need not say, but I may think," snapped up Mr. Black; " and, with regard to the question you put to me some time since, all I have got to remark is this—I will work with you, and for you and myself, if you will let me; but there is a limit to all things. I cannot stand being bullied and interfered with. Let me work the company my own way, and I will take what amount of advice you choose to give, and act on it if I can. I am a good servant, if I am let alone—interfere with this, that, and the other, and I am apt to turn restive. If you take the right way with me, you will not find me unreasonable; but I tell you fairly to begin with, that though a child might lead, the devil himself should not drive me."

"I must advertise for an intelligent three-year-old, then," laughed Mr. Stewart, "for I shall certainly not attempt driving you. Only, I mean to have my way in some things, remember. I am a little like you, Mr. Black—averse to being crossed; so it will be better for us to agree to go the same road, rather than always be pulling contrary ways. You will bear in mind what I said about our company being made a refuge, and not repeat such a mistake. I shall look in again after Christmas; meantime, allow me to wish you the compliments of the season."

" Thank you; same to you, sir," answered Mr. Black, forced to accept the civility, but by no means mollified by it.

" I hope the new year may prove a prosperous one to us all," said Mr. Stewart, meditatively, looking into his hat.

" I hope so too," the promoter agreed; " it shall not be for want of any exertions on my part if the company fail."

" Fail," repeated Mr. Stewart; " fail! it shall not fail! Conducted with ordinary prudence, it should be a perfect mine of wealth. There is scarcely a public bakery in England which has not paid the most enormous dividends; and what is the field in any county or provincial town in comparison to that which is open for us in London? Three millions of bread-eaters, and not a large bakery to supply them!"

" You may remember that I make a somewhat similar observation in the prospectus," remarked Mr. Black, not sorry to have an opportunity of indirectly accusing Mr. Stewart of plagiarism.

" Did you? How very singular! Is it copyright? If so, I will not infringe again. And that reminds me what induces you to stick the Mount Cashell motto at the heads of each advertisement."

"I suppose the motto was in existence before the Mount Cashells were thought of," retorted Mr. Black. "It is none the worse for their having used it, is it?"

"It is none the better," was the reply; "still," went on Mr. Stewart, "the prospectus, as a whole, does you credit. It is very moderate in its tone—a great matter in these days of bounce and swagger; and that allusion to the 'Give us bread and the games' is rather neat. I like the stamp motto also, 'Sweet and wholesome.' Altogether, that Latin of yours is a good idea."

"The idea was mine, but not the Latin," answered Mr. Black, frankly. "I do not pretend to be much of a scholar myself; I had something else to do when I was young than pore over any book, unless, indeed, it might be a day-book; but I know even the appearance of learning has an effect on the general public, and so I begged Dudley to look me up one or two appropriate quotations. He is a gentleman, you know—been to college, and all that sort of thing."

"They do not sell brains at college, it appears, however, though they may learning," remarked Mr. Stewart, drily; after which speech, intended, evidently, as a delicate compliment to Arthur Dudley's understanding, the great director put his hat on his head, and said "Good afternoon" to Mr. Black, and, walking out of the office, took his way westward through Cloak and Trinity Lanes, thinking as he went, "That is a sharp, clever fellow. Now I wonder if he can and will be honest, even to answer his own purpose."

Meanwhile, the subject of this speculation stood shaking his clenched fist after Mr. Stewart.

"I wish to God I dare have kicked the old humbug up Cannon Street," he said in his rage, quite out loud. "I should not mind paying a hundred pounds to have the pleasure of telling the cursed upstart that I don't care a damn for him, or his connection, or his standing, or anything about him. Here have I had all the trouble, all the anxiety, all the work, while my gentleman was amusing himself doing the grand in foreign countries; and then, when I, after having stood the racket, began to hope the rest would be smooth sailing, down he comes with his capital, and sweeps away all chance of profit. Capital, indeed; damn capital, say I !"

Thus the man whose life had been one long struggle to gain capital, who was never weary of writing prospectus after prospectus in order to prove that without capital nothing good or great ever had been, or ever would be, accomplished; the ostensible object of whose existence it was to demonstrate that individual exertion was useless; that it was only the united wealth of a number of individuals which could hope to effect large results; the actual end of whose labours—could those labours have been carried out according to the programme he had arranged—was to exterminate all small tradesmen, all struggling merchants — almost unconsciously paraphrased the sense of Mr. Raidsford's lamentation.

Great wits and little wits, we are assured, often-times jump together, and on this occasion, certainly, the man of large resources and the man of none expressed nearly identical opinions.

"The concentration of capital will be the ruin of England," said Mr. Raidsford, who felt how such a concentration might have neutralized his own efforts to rise in the world.

"Damn capital!" said Mr. Black, smarting under Mr. Stewart's insolence; "it is capital, and nothing but capital, which enables these fellows to give themselves such airs."

"But the game is not finished yet," added the promoter, next instant; "when it is, Mr. Stewart, you will perhaps find out to your cost which of us rises the winner."

CHAPTER VI.

HOLLY BERRIES.

THE accident at Berrie Down brought, during the course of the few weeks preceding Christmas, an unprecedented number of visitors to the Hollow. Never before in the memory of any individual connected with the establishment had so many carriages, driven up to the door in the course of one day as was the case when once news of Lally's precarious state came to be bruited abroad.

People who had never called on Mrs. Dudley now called to inquire after her child, and there had to be a piece of cork fastened under the knocker, and some baize tied round the clapper of the bell, in order to prevent Heather being maddened by the incessant rat-tat-tat and ting-ting-ting of her neighbours' grand footmen.

Very little social courtesy had been extended to Mrs. Dudley since her marriage. Long before her advent, the Dudleys had dropped off the visiting lists of their more aristocratic acquaintances, and no one felt much inclined to take steps towards reviving the old intimacy when Arthur Dudley brought home to the Hollow a wife of whom no one knew anything, who might, in fact, be "anybody"—as Mrs. Poole Seymour, the great lady of North Kemms, vaguely expressed herself.

When society does not take notice of a woman on the occasion of her marriage, it is difficult for any member composing it subsequently to repair that omission; and thus, although there was scarcely a lady in the three parishes who would not willingly enough have extended her countenance to Mrs. Dudley, and although most persons' consciences pricked them when they passed the Hollow, or met the pretty woman and her children, and the brothers and sisters-in-law whom she had so speedily tamed and civilized, in Berrie Down Lane, still Heather's circle of acquaintances had remained extremely limited, and might have remained so for many a year longer, had not Lally's accident broken the conventional ice, and brought, as I have said, visitors and kind inquiries to Berrie Down in abundance.

The excitement produced by the little girl's illness and danger was, indeed, something astonishing. Mothers had a fellow-feeling for the poor creature who sat—so the doctor reported—day and night by her little girl's side. Those who were childless had perhaps even a keener, because a more imaginative and sentimental sympathy in the matter. Gentlemen, as a rule, admired Heather, and regretted that any trouble should fall upon her; and, added to all these causes of compassion, there was a strong feeling in the small community round about Berrie Down that Mrs. Dudley was a victim—an unappreciated victim, moreover; that she must have had a hard time of it with those boys and girls, and that "proud, useless husband," and that it was quite time somebody took her up and made her position more endurable.

The world's pity is usually abundant in inverse proportion to the necessity that exists for it to be vouchsafed at all.

Certainly, Heather did not consider the five

brothers and sisters a cause for repining, nor had she ever murmured because she and her husband often found it a hard struggle to make the two ends of their income meet.

If, of late, she had occasionally wept over any paragraph in her life's story, those tears were never shed in public—of their bitterness she never complained to any created being.

Her happiness the world could not mar, her grief the world could not cure; and, perhaps for both these reasons, and also because she felt that society was by no means an inexpensive luxury, she did not respond to the advances now made with so much alacrity as the ladies of the three parishes thought she might have done under the circumstances.

"Under the circumstances" meant, that, although they—the ladies—had neglected Mrs. Dudley at first, still they had availed themselves of the earliest opportunity which offered of making amends to her for their former want of attention.

They were willing to forget all the years during which the Dudleys had voluntarily put themselves on one side, if the Dudleys would forget those years likewise; but Heather did not, as has been stated, appear unduly elated by the somewhat tardy honour which was now sought to be thrust upon her. It was not in her nature to be unthankful or ungracious; but her mind was troubled about her child, she said, and she trusted visitors would excuse her coming down to them.

Thus Bessie Ormson and Agnes Dudley were in the habit of repulsing great ladies day after. day; but, somehow, the autocrats of their various ilks did not take these apologetic messages in bad part,—rather, on the contrary, they professed their anxiety that poor dear Mrs. Dudley should not leave her little girl, and appeared quite content to hear the story of the accident from the lips of other members of Squire Dudley's family.

Hitherto, most decidedly, the younger Dudleys had been rather a trouble to the minds of those exalted persons who occasionally deigned to discuss Berrie Down Hollow and the persons who dwelt there.

They were regarded as a species of fungus which had been permitted to grow upon and disfigure a very old and a very good tree. Grandchildren were they of an alderman—a poor alderman, be it remembered, who had not even thought it worth

his while to recognise the honour birth had conferred on him and his, by leaving a sufficient
amount of money behind to patch up the broken
fortunes of the Dudleys of Berrie Down.

If trade were to be tolerated at all, it could only
be tolerated for the sake of the wealth it brought to
aristocratic, but empty coffers.

In itself, like a servant, it was an evil; but like
a servant also, if it did its work, its presence might
be both tolerated and approved.

If it failed to perform its appointed task—if it
grew poor and pretentious, like its betters, then the
sooner it was stamped out the better.

A poor alderman seemed in the eyes of those
great people nothing more nor less than an arrant
impostor. Of course, any gentleman marrying the
daughter of such a person would conclude she had
money, and for her not to have money was a downright deception.

Then for her to have five children. "Those
kind of vulgar women always have tribes of children, my dear," said Mrs. Poole Seymour, who was
childless, to the Honourable Augusta Baldwin (Lord
Kemms' aunt), who was popularly supposed never to

have had an offer.   " If poor Major Dudley had lived much longer, there is no telling how many sons and daughters might have been left for his heir to support.   Shocking I call it.   You remember, the first wife had only one child, and this present Mrs. Dudley but two.   Quite enough, to my mind—just a nice number; but as for those five other creatures, it is perfectly heartbreaking to think of any man being burdened with them."

This was the bird's-eye view of the question which society from an exalted position was good enough to take.

When, however, society condescended to a nearer inspection, affairs assumed a somewhat different aspect.   The Dudley girls were not uncouth young women, with large bones, rough hair, loud voices, and red hands; rather they were, to borrow from Mrs. Poole Seymour once more, decidedly pleasing girls—very nice and unaffected in their manners, and irreproachable as to their accent.   Altogether, a call at Berrie Down grew to be considered an agreeable object for a morning drive.   The ladies of the three parishes were, perhaps, a trifle weary of each other, and liked, moreover, having something to do.

Fruit and flowers, game, picture-books, dolls, toys, came daily to the Hollow, together with compliments and kind inquiries. Callers arrived also, assured that some day Heather herself would become visible, and also very certain that half an hour at Berrie Down passed more rapidly than ten minutes anywhere else.

Bessie did her best to amuse the great people, and the great people were pleased to approve her efforts. "You and your sisters, really must come over and stay with me," Mrs. Poole Seymour was good enough at last to declare; and then Bessie had to explain she was not a Miss Dudley at all,—only a cousin wishful to help Mrs. Dudley at that trying period. A "sort of nurse," added Bessie, mischievously, whereupon Agnes Dudley observed, "A very pearl of nurses; I do not know what we should have done without her;" at which little speech Mrs. Poole Seymour smiled graciously, and said they were good, sweet girls, of whom she trusted she should yet have the pleasure of seeing a great deal.

"She has all the trust, and all the pleasure on her side, then," remarked Bessie, after their visitor departed; but, in spite of this depreciating observation, there can be no question but that Miss Ormson liked playing hostess—that she delighted in trying her strength and testing her power on grand ladies who were to the manner born, and never seemed disturbed or put out by any circumstance, or any person.

Another thing pleased her also—the vain coquettish puss—namely, to run up to her room after the various callers had departed, and looking in the glass consider how much prettier—how much more graceful she was than any of them.

Mrs. Crompton Raidsford was amongst the earliest of Mrs. Dudley's visitors. No one, not even the Earl's daughter, who married Mr. Plimpton, of Thornfield—a man commonly believed to be rolling in wealth—came in such style to Berrie Down as the contractor's wife.

She had the shortest distance to drive of any lady in the neighbourhood, yet she arrived in a great chariot, drawn by a pair of horses, seventeen hands high if they were an inch, with coachman and footman on the box, and another footman behind.

As Bessie subsequently remarked, " Anybody

might have thought the Lord Mayor of London had come out in his state carriage to visit us. I really felt quite subdued by such unnecessary magnificence."

"And if you only saw Mrs. Raidsford, Heather," she went on ; "if you could only imagine the mass of satin, and velvet, and sable, and pretension and vulgarity, which descended, assisted by two foot-men, from that chariot, you would be astonished to think Mr. Raidsford has lived with her so long. I never did behold such a woman. I dare not look at Agnes while she was talking. Do you think I could at first imagine whom she meant by 'your gentleman,' or conceive why she wanted to know what sized nursery you had ? I consider it was most clever of Agnes to interrupt me when I was going to say I could get a rule from Cuthbert and measure it for her. How came you to guess, Aggy, that was her way of inquiring how many children Heather had ? She said she hoped you would not think she had condescended in coming over so soon—"

" What !" exclaimed Heather in astonishment.

"She meant intruded, I believe," explained Bessie, " for that Mr. Raidsford had never given her a moment's peace about calling ever since he heard of the collusion your little girl had met with. I may safely say," proceeded Bessie, " that she did not use a single long word in its right sense. She informed us—talking of ghosts, that she was not supercilious—that if we would come over to Moorlands any day she would be very glad to show us the apiary Mr. R. had built for British birds; that her young ladies were not much of ones for pedestrian exercise, that they preferred walking to riding, only their ' papar' thought it was well for them to be learned how to do it. She told us her nerves never would have been strong enough for her to do anything in that way; in fact, it always put her heart in her mouth to see Lord Kemms a leaping of that Black Knight of his over the fossil on the lawn. If she mentioned Lord Kemms once during the time she was here," went on Bessie, " she did sixty times. That is the worst of a man rising; he has to carry his wife a dead weight, up with him. Well, there must be some of her to be some of all sorts— so let us rest and be thankful."

Utterly astonished was Arthur at sight of the visitors who came to inquire concerning the health of his eldest born.

" Leonard might have broken every bone in his body before they would have offered any such civility," he grumbled; but Bessie bade him " hush —sh—sh—"

" It was really your good child Leonard, Arthur, who pushed her in," she said; " and if we have been wise enough to keep that fact in the background, I pray you not to be ungrateful. It was poor Heather's sinner who fell into the water, but it was your saint who was the cause of her doing so. And it is natural such a catastrophe should bring wives and mothers to Berrie Down. It brought me, so you ought not to be surprised at anything after that."

"It was very kind of you, Bessie," answered Squire Dudley; but, nevertheless, he refused to see their visitors, and it was long before the honours of Berrie Down were done by Heather in person.

Then, indeed, Mrs. Poole Seymour, and the Honourable Augusta Baldwin, Mrs. Plimpton, and Mrs. Carroll, and Mrs. Raidsford, and Mrs. Lynford, and Mrs. Hulst, and a multitude of other morning callers, professed themselves charmed, and wondered how it happened they could have resided for so long a time within visiting distance of Berrie Down without knowing that dear, sweet, gentle Mrs. Dudley.

"Anything prettier than Mrs. Dudley and her little girl," opined society, "had never been exhibited at the Royal Academy;" and, certainly, in those days, both mother and child were very touching—Heather pathetic, with pale thin face and anxious eyes; Lally so easily tired, so soon wearied, even with fresh toys and strange faces.

"Oo dood to Lally," she said to Mrs. Poole Seymour when that lady bought her a doll's house furnished complete, and would have had the child play with and enjoy it; "oo dood to Lally, but Lally tired mamma—tell lady—Lally's very bad¿"

There was not a woman who went up in due time to the room where Lally lay that left it with dry eyes. Even Mrs. Raidsford declared the scene was "quite effective." As for Mrs. Poole Seymour, she was never weary of bringing over toys for the child, which the poor little creature always clutched with weak avidity, and then next moment almost wearily relinquished.

There were two spirits in poor Lally then; the spirit of health and the spirit of sickness, the spirit of her former self, and the spirit which entered into her body as she rose for the last time struggling for life in the cold waters of Mr. Scrotter's pond. The first was all eagerness, excitement, vivacity; the last was languid, weary, inactive; the first hastened her pulses, sent the blood to her cheeks, loaded her tongue with eager words, and tipped her fingers with quicksilver; the second laid a depressing weight on her heart, caused the unspoken words to die away on her white lips, drew the bright colour from her face, checked the impulses of the little hands, and caused the tired head to be laid on her mother's breast almost before the new toys were examined,—the latest wonder in doll creation critically inspected.

"Put 'em away," she was wont to say with the air of a matron of forty, " put 'em away, Lally look at 'em by-and-by."

But by-and-by came and went,—came and went without bringing much more inclination to Lally to inspect her new possessions.

The loveliest doll on earth could not have retained her attention very long in the days of which I am writing. She would look at it for a moment and then turn her eyes wearily away. "Lally not well," that was the burden of the song then; "Ma,—Lally not well."

"But you are better, my pet," Heather was wont to say. "You are not very bad now, Lally."

"No, but Lally not well;" and then mother and doctor and friends would look at each other and declare "she is much better, and the spring will do wonders for her."

Of that spring and of the summer Lally might have been said to rave. Each morning when she opened her eyes, she would ask between sleeping and waking, "Bessie, are the leaves come yet?" or "are the trees green? Is it spring now?"

"Nonsense, puss," Bessie always answered, "Christmas has not come yet; you are to get well, you know, and be carried downstairs to eat your plum pudding. Little girls who sham sickness are not to have any good things at all. You are to be taken into the drawing-room and kissed under the misletoe—kissed till you are black and blue, you bad child, for all the trouble and anxiety you have caused us."

Whereupon Lally would declare she "wadn't

bad tild, and she wouldn't be tissed back and bue;
Lally has had more tisses than ze liked these days;
Lally tired of ladies tissing of her."

"You little ungrateful monkey!"

"Big fat ooman tissed Lally, and hurt her with
her beard," the child complained, "and Lally did
not like her sweet-sweets; they were nasty."

"You ought not to have had any, you know, you
dreadful child!"

"Lally ought; Lally would like some this minute,
if they was dood, and not mortar. Issy said they
were mortar, and that Mrs. Aidsford had no bussi-
ness to bring them: but Issy says wicked things,
and Lally isn't to 'tend to her."

Having finished which speech, Lilian Dudley
nestled her head in her pillow, and thought over her
various visitors.

"I'd like to have Muff," she said at last, as a
consolatory conclusion; and, accordingly, Muff was
brought; and from that day forth the cat rarely
left its little mistress's side. By some mysterious
means, the creature seemed to understand there was
a terrible fight going on in the silent room, and it
would lie for hours quietly beside the child, purring

vigorously, never moving, unless Lally said, tenderly, " poor titty," or " poor puss," in which case it would open its eyes and blink at her gratefully, or else march backwards and forwards over her breast, rubbing sides, and head, and tail against the pinched, changed face of the little child.

There was nothing much sadder, in those days, than the contemplation of Lally and " pussens," as she styled her cat.

There was the meek, unassuming, yet intense sympathy of the dumb creature, not unmixed, it might be, with a perfect appreciation of the physical comforts which Lally's illness provided for her. There was, on the other hand, the irritable and unreasonable affection of the higher creature—the exacting fondness of a mistress who expected Muff continually to get up out of her sleep, to rub against and make much of her.

Which Muff did—greatly to her credit, as I consider.

A dozen times in an hour the cat was roused from her slumber, with invariably the same result; and, sleepy or not sleepy, she was always expected, if Lally wished that she should do so, to fold her

paws, lie quiet, put down her head, commence purring, and so wander into dreamland once again.

"Poor pussens, poor tittens, poor Muff!" and so
mistress and cat would fall to rest, mutually caress-
ing each other; and sometimes Bessie, watching
the pair, would turn her head aside and cry
silently.

They were gathering holly berries in those days;
and Lally had longed to go out and watch the holly
being cut "in Berrie Down Lane, and just round
about, ma," she said; but in this matter Heather was
firm. "My pet must not put her little face outside
the doors till spring comes," she answered; and then
Lally very piteously asked, "Will spring be long,
ma,—will spring be long?"

"Look at the beautiful dress I have made for
Lally's own self," said Bessie on Christmas-eve—
holding up a little frock of white cashmere, which
she had bound and trimmed, and decked out
prettily with light blue ribbon. "My child is to be
dressed up in all this loveliness to-night, and carried
down in Bessie's arms, to say to mamma and papa
'merry Christmas, happy new year.' Lally won't be
awake soon enough in the morning to say all that

long sentence. Would Lally like to be dressed, and go now?"

Lally conceiving that she would, the grand dress was slipped on over her little night-gown, then a soft blue shawl was thrown round her neck, and thus attired, with her head resting on Bessie's shoulder, Lally put in her first appearance in the family circle.

"My darling, my darling!" Heather said; and she stood up white and trembling as she spoke.

"Is that my little girl?" Arthur exclaimed, making a movement to take her, in which he was restrained, however, by Lally's statement that she was not to be hurt. "Lally's been very sore, pa," she explained. "Merry Chris-mes, dood new year!"

"That is not it," whispered Bessie, giving her a little admonitory shake,—"happy."

"Ma, happy Chris-mes, merry new year!" and the little creature made the round of the family, not forgetting Master Marsden, whom Bessie reluctantly allowed to kiss her. Surreptitiously and remorsefully that young gentleman conveyed into Lally's hand five or six marbles, which had been secreted about his person.

"They are for you," he whispered; and the gift

Lally religiously carried up-stairs, falling asleep with the precious stones laid in a heap beside her.

"Ver pret," she said, pointing to the great branch of holly, with its red berries glowing among the glossy leaves, which Bessie had suspended over the top of her little bed, " ver—pret."

" Yes, my darling, they are ver--ver pret," answered Bessie, while she took off Lally's finery, and laid her down among the snowy napery; and when all that was done, and Lally was tucked up for the night, Bessie took her seat beside the bed, and told the child, as well as she could, what event the holly berries were hung there to commemorate; told her how, more than eighteen centuries before, the wise men came to worship at Bethlehem, and how the star had gone before them, and stood over the manger where Jesus was laid.

"That is why we hang our houses with holly branches, Lally," Bessie went on, " because to-morrow is the birthday of One who loved us all exceedingly. Do you understand me, pet?"

" Iss," was the reply, " Lally does; Lally heard all that before long ago, that is why we have plum-pudden too."

Rather disheartened at this view of the question, Bessie observed, that when people were glad they prepare a feast, and "make merry," and that plum-pudding happened to be part of the good things provided at Christmas.

"Did He have dood tings?" Lally immediately inquired, with the terrible perception of the incongruous, which makes it so difficult to talk to children on serious subjects in connection with their daily life.

Altogether, it seemed to Bessie that she had better have left her religious instruction alone; but she had gone too far to recede, and accordingly she answered that "He had been poorly lodged, poorly fed, evilly treated while He remained on earth; that though He had done so much for men, men had used Him despitefully, and mocked and forsaken Him. But He loved little children, Lally," finished Bessie, "and so, when you look at the holly berries, you must always think of Him. He was so good, Lally, that Child born eighteen hundred years ago. He was so good!"

"Are you dood, Bessie?" asked the little creature.

"No, my darling, I am not; I wish I were; oh! Lally, I wish I were!"

"You are dood to Lally," was the encouraging reply. "Bessie, I do love 'oo; thing to I, please; thing I to thleep."

But Bessie refused to sing at all till Lally said "sleep" properly.

"Seep dere den," Lally exclaimed in a tone of such triumph that Bessie was fain to kiss her a dozen times ere commencing one of those dear old Christmas carols that one never hears now-a-days, that went out of fashion with the Christmas frosts and snows.

By the time the strain was ended, Lally had fallen asleep; but through the night she wakened and asked Agnes, who sat beside her bed, to tell her more about the Child.

"What child, dear?" said Agnes, who thought she was dreaming or wandering.

"It is His birthday, you know; the Child;" and then Agnes knew what she meant, and told her stories about Him and His goodness till Lally said plaintively, "I wis He was here now, Aggy."

"I wish He were, my darling, for He would make

you better in a moment," Agnes answered, sorrow-fully.

"Agnes!"—it was Heather coming into the room with a loose dressing-gown thrown around her that made Agnes turn at this point,—" He is here, and He will make my child well, if it seemeth Him good. I prayed for her all the time she was so very ill, as it would have been impossible for me to have prayed, had I not felt He was with me, standing near; but I tried not to pray too much, dear, lest in granting my petition He should punish me for it."

And so mother and aunt talked while the child dropped off into slumber once again, and so the Christmas morning dawned—fine, and clear, and bright; and the holly berries looked red and warm as the December sun peered through the windows of the Hollow, and found everything there in due order for a quiet, happy Christmas.

The child was not well, but she was out of danger, and Heather felt she must that day go to church and thank God for delivering her darling from the lions—for giving her back from the very jaws of death, to life, and hope, to parents, and friends.

CHAPTER VII.

GONE.

IT was a lovely morning, and every one was going to walk over to Fifield church except Laura, who had almost tearfully entreated to be left in charge of Lally.

"I love her as much as any of you," she said, "and still I have the least to do with her."

So it was settled that Laura should remain at home, and all the rest proceed along Berrie Down Lane,—up which we walked slowly and lingeringly in the first chapter in this book—to Fifield.

A large party—for, although the intended festivities had been given up, and no visitors were invited to Berrie Down Hollow, still, the Dudleys themselves made a goodly number — eight, including Bessie—who looked pale and tired when she came into the drawing-room, "dressed in all her best;" so shrieked Harry Marsden—and ready to go to church.

"Mayn't I go too?" asked that young gentleman, pulling at Heather's dress; "I'd like the walk as well as anybody."

"Do you think it is only for the sake of the walk we are going to church, Harry?" asked Agnes, virtuously drawing on her gloves as she spoke.

"How should I know? Bessie's likely going for the sake of the young men; that's what pa says takes all girls to church," answered the *enfant terrible*.

"Well, I daresay Mrs. Dudley will not object to your seeing whether that is what we go for," said Bessie. "I will brush your hair and put you to rights, for you are a perfect scarecrow now."

And thus it was settled Master Marsden should accompany the party; and Alick, home for Christmas, had not a chance given him of looking at Agnes to see how she took Harry's remark about the object for which young ladies went to church.

"What had taken her to North Kemms," he wondered; "whom could the man be they had met there? what his connection with Bessie?"

These questions Alick stood striving vainly to answer, while Master Marsden was being brushed and made look respectable by Bessie Ormson.

"I am as good as a mother to you, Harry," she said.

"I am sure you are; but that's not saying much," answered the boy. "Mine has always a headache, and is constantly telling us not to make a noise. Noise, indeed! Women can make enough noise themselves, when they want to."

"Do not say 'want to,' Harry, it is vulgar."

"No more vulgar than you are," he replied. "I shall talk as I like. What is good enough for pa ought to be good enough for you."

"It is a fortunate thing for both of us that I am not your pa, as you call him," Bessie answered, "for I should shake you to death some day. Now, are you ready, or are you going to keep us waiting all day?"

"You think you look so nice in that bonnet," Harry sneered, "that you want to be off like a flash of lightning. You are none so pretty, some people think, though Harcourt, as my papa says, does imagine there is nobody like you. Pa says he would not marry you. I heard pa tell ma so, not a week before I came here."

" I can't wonder at that," Bessie replied; " your papa probably finds he has married one too many of the family already."

But this side stroke Master Marsden seemed unable perfectly to understand; wherefore he asked Bessie what she meant; in reply to which question he received the information that " children should not ask too many questions; and that, if he intended going with them to Fifield church, it was time he got his cap and went downstairs."

In acknowledgment of all this instruction, Harry, pulling a face at Bessie, that young lady forthwith unceremoniously marched him off and gave him in charge of Cuthbert, who grumbled a little over the trust.

Human nature is much the same on Christmas as on any other day in the week, and every creature in Berrie Down—Heather herself not excepted—felt Harry Marsden to be a burden and a tax.

Never before — never, Heather thought, had Berrie Down Lane looked so lovely as it did on that morning when they all paced it side by side. She had not been out for weeks previously, and the very branches of the trees seemed to bend and greet her as she passed.

'There were few leaves, and there were no wild flowers, yet the banks and hedgerows looked warm and pleasant, the ivy was trailing over the sward and twining fresh and green round the roots of the elms and beeches; the spruce laurel put forth its glossy foliage between the bare boughs of the thorn, and its bluish-black berries formed a contrast to those of the holly, red and glowing in the sunshine.

Everything looked fair and lovely to Heather on that Christmas morning. Arthur had been so kind to her for weeks past, had never grumbled about Lally's illness, nor complained concerning the child having occupied too much of her time and thoughts.

Alick was back amongst them—not much changed by his sojourn in town—good, and considerate, and helpful as ever. He talked hopefully of a vacant situation in Messrs. Elser's office, which he thought Cuthbert might fill; and Heather's secret desire for many a day previously had been that when Cuthbert went forth into the world it might be under Alick's auspices.

She did not feel quite so certain of the one boy as of the other; she did not think that as Cuthbert grew up she could manage him without Alick's aid. He was more uncertain in his temper, less to be depended on in any way, weaker for good, stronger for evil than his brother. Altogether, Heather desired that Alick should have the supervision of him; and, behold, there was already a chance of the desire being gratified.

Then Lally was better; though not yet strong, she was certainly better, and the girls were well; even Bessie made no complaint, though Heather thought she looked a trifle pale in her pretty bonnet, made of violet velvet, which was about the most becoming colour and material possible to the complexion of that young belle, Miss Ormson.

"What a shame, dear, that Gilbert is not with us," Heather had laughingly said the same morning, standing under the misletoe. "Let me kiss you for him."

"Kiss me for yourself, Heather," Bessie answered, colouring up to her very temples, "but not for him."

"And why not for him?" asked Heather.

" I will tell you to-morrow, not to-day," was the reply. " To-morrow, perhaps."

And then, irresistibly, there came back to Heather's mind that passage in " Elizabeth, or the Exiles of Siberia," where Elizabeth, repeating the word " to-morrow," sighs.

" You look pale, Bessie," Heather remarked, when they had almost reached the foot of Berrie Down Lane. " Are you getting tired, dear ?"

" I do not feel very well," Bessie answered; " I think I will go back again, if you have no objection."

Immediately, every one offered to return with her, even Harry Marsden, who, being debarred from throwing stones at the birds, was beginning to feel weary of the walk.

" I do not mind going to church." " Let me walk back with you." " No, I will go." " No, you have not been out for ever so long." " Let me "— " me"—" me."

All of which polite offers Bessie declined, saying, " if any one insisted on returning with her, she should walk on to church."

" I am not ill," she finished, " I am only tired; when I get home, I shall lie down and be as bright by

the time you come back as any of you. Good-bye,
—*au revoir!*"—and with that she kissed her hand,
and commenced slowly retracing her steps—Heather
turning every now and then to watch her progress.

The farther the distance between them became,
the silenter grew Heather. She felt a nameless
anxiety about Bessie,—an anxiety which she could
neither conquer nor analyze, but which, nevertheless,
increased until when, almost within sight of Fifield
church, she remarked to her husband that she
really thought she must return home also.

"I am uneasy about Bessie," she said; "the girl
certainly did not look well."

"Pooh!" exclaimed Arthur, "she is only a little
tired. It would vex her if you went home now; I
should not think of doing such a thing, I really
should not, Heather."

And so Heather was persuaded not to follow
after Bessie, but go on to church.

"You will find her well enough on our return,"
remarked Arthur; and his prophecy proved correct,
for Bessie met them at the gate looking bright and
happy, and with as rich a colour as she had ever
boasted mantling in her cheeks.

" Hollo ! you've been painting," cried out Master Marsden. "Hasn't she, Alick? nobody's face was ever like that, without paint."

"Harry, I really shall have to write to your mamma if you make such rude remarks," said Heather, rebukingly. "And so," she added, addressing Bessie, "you do feel quite well again? I felt so uneasy after you left us that I should have turned, had it not been for Arthur's remonstrance."

"I am glad he did remonstrate," answered Bessie, "it would have been a real grief to me if you had come home on my account. I felt a little tired, that was all, and I am quite rested now."

So, indeed, it seemed, for never had Bessie been so gay as on that Christmas afternoon. And she was very sweet too, as well as gay; she uttered no sharp speeches; she was ready to play at cat's-cradle with Leonard, and even refrained from scolding when Harry Marsden, who must needs take a hand in that scientific game also, tore her lace sleeve to shreds.

She made herself agreeable to Arthur likewise, talking to him, while Heather was upstairs, concerning London, and her father's business, and her father's anxieties, and the Squire's own prospects, as quietly and sensibly, her cousin subsequently declared, as her mother might have done.

"And I think, Heather, she must be very fond of her father," Arthur informed his wife; "for once when she was speaking about him, and how hard he worked, and of how little help her brothers were to him, her voice quite shook, and the tears came into her eyes. I had not given Bessie credit for so much feeling."

"She is a dear, sweet girl," Heather answered. "I am glad she did not insist, as I feared she might, on sitting up with Lally. She is completely worn out, I think. Did you notice how pale she turned when she was bidding us good-night?"

Other people beside Heather had observed this pallor. Mrs. Piggott, who, making a grievous complaint concerning Priscilla Dobbin's shortcomings and habit of always being out of the way when wanted, was silenced by the sight of Bessie's wan face, and by Bessie's entreaty for her not to be hard on Priscilla.

"She was with me a long time, you know, Mrs. Piggott, to-day," she said; "I did not feel very well when I returned this morning, and Prissy put away my bonnet, and did a few other things for me that I was not inclined to do for myself."

"There, there, Miss, don't say another word, but go away to bed; you look like a ghost this minute; you have been trying to kill yourself lately, that is my opinion; but, please God, we will all turn round now."

"Where shall we turn to, Mrs. Piggott?" asked Bessie, with a smile, and then she re-crossed the hall and ascended the stairs to her own room, only pausing for a moment ere she went, to ask Alick if he would take a letter up to town for her on the following morning.

"It is to papa, and he will receive it earlier if you post it in London. Thank you. I will leave it on the hall-table to-night. Good-bye, Alick, good-bye!" and Alick imagined she pressed his hand tighter than ever she had done before, and that there was a very plaintive tone in her voice as she uttered that word, "Good-bye."

Later on in the night, when every one except Lucy Dudley, who sat up with Lally, was supposed to be in bed, Bessie stole into the nursery, "to have another peep at her child," she said.

"You ought to have been asleep long ago," Lucy remarked, rebukingly; but Bessie explained she had been writing to her father a very long letter on an important subject, which Alick was going to take to town with him.

"About your marriage?" Lucy inquired, and Bessie answered, "Yes."

"If we talk any more, we shall waken Lally," the girl added. "Good-night, Lucy—good-night, my bad child—my poor little Lally!"

And stooping, she put her lips to Lally's hand, which lay outside the coverlet, and kissed it softly. When she lifted her head, Lucy saw that her eyes were full of tears.

"Bessie, Bessie, darling, what is the matter?" she whispered, putting her arms round her cousin's neck, and striving to detain her; but Bessie gently disengaged herself from the embrace, and saying, "we shall waken Lally; there is nothing the matter with me," left the room—her face buried in her handkerchief, sobbing, sobbing as she went. Lucy would have followed her, but Bessie motioned her not to do so. Then, gliding noiselessly along the passage, she entered her own room, and Agnes heard the key turned in the lock.

Some hours afterwards, when Heather, as was her custom, came to relieve the watcher, Lucy expressed her fear that Bessie could not be well. "She cried so bitterly," the girl explained.

Hearing this, Mrs. Dudley went to Bessie's door, and quietly turned the handle.

Contrary to her expectations, the bolt was not drawn inside, and she stepped into the apartment.

In the darkness she stood, holding her breath and listening. Bessie was asleep. Heather heard the regular respiration of what she considered sound slumber, and felt satisfied.

"I do not imagine she can be ill," Mrs. Dudley remarked, on her return to Lucy. "She is sleeping quietly enough now, at all events. Tell me, dear," she added, "have you heard any noise at all during the night? I fancied I caught a sound something like footsteps crunching on the gravel, and got up to see. Arthur said it was all my fancy. Did you hear anything?"

"No," Lucy replied, "nothing whatever. Bessie was downstairs again, you know, leaving out that letter for Alick to take to town; but she was very quiet. I do not think you could have heard her."

"It was my fancy, I suppose," remarked Heather. "I have felt restless and nervous all the night long. I was quite glad when four o'clock struck to get up. Now, go to bed, Lucy, or you will feel ill for want of sleep."

"No likelihood of that," Lucy answered, suppressing a yawn, however, as she spoke, and went off, leaving mother and child alone.

Sitting there quite alone with her little girl, the restlessness of which Heather had complained returned upon her with double force. She tried to read; she fetched her work-basket, and commenced sewing; she went and stood by the window looking out into the darkness, and longed for five o'clock, when there would come some sounds of life about the house. It was a still, cold morning, pitch dark. Not a dog barked—not a leaf stirred. The silence was almost insupportable, and Heather felt it to be so, as she left the window and returned to Lally's side.

Still, the child slept quietly; and now Heather's thoughts reverted to Bessie. What could be the matter with the girl? Why had she been crying the previous night? Why did she so persistently ignore Mr. Harcourt's very existence? How did it happen that the time for her marriage seemed no nearer now than it had done in the summer?

That Mr. Harcourt was a devoted correspondent, Heather knew by the evidence of her own eyes. Scarcely a morning passed without the post-bag bringing a long epistle from him to his affianced wife. Bessie's acknowledgments of these epistles were despatched at much longer and more uncertain intervals; but then Bessie did not profess to be a good correspondent. "She hated letter-writing and letter-writers," she openly declared; so that her negligence in this particular proved nothing. Besides, her time had been much occupied with Lally, and altogether——

As she reached this point in her mental argument, Mrs. Dudley heard a sound as though a door were being softly opened and closed at the end of the corridor. With that nervous fear upon her, which seems so often the advance courier of some disaster, the messenger spurring on to tell us of the approach of misfortune, Heather went out into the passage and listened. Yes, there was some one moving stealthily and cautiously in the direction of the back staircase—a woman, for Mrs. Dudley could hear the skirt of her dress brushing against the wall as she stole along.

It could not be any of the servants, because they had no business in that part of the house ;—their sleeping-rooms being in the roof, and access to those apartments only possible by means of the back staircase which opened out of the front kitchen.

There was a door of communication, however, between the long south corridor, where the principal bedchambers were situated, and the other portion of the house ; and this door Heather now heard close softly, as the first had done.

Satisfied that Bessie must be ill and about to seek Mrs. Piggott's apartment, Heather hurried after ; but when she came to try to open the door, it resisted all her efforts. As a rule, the key remained on the side next the main staircase. Now, Heather found it had been removed, and the door locked from within. Not knowing what all this could mean, she went back to Lally's room, took a candle, and, descending into the hall, made her way along a passage which led in the direction of the offices. Crossing the front kitchen, she opened the door which led towards the back staircase, and there on the last step stood Priscilla Dobbin.

" What are you doing? where are you going?" asked her mistress.

"I was coming down to look at the clock, ma'am," answered the girl.

" You have just left Miss Ormson's room—is she ill ?"

" No, ma'am, not as I know of. She told me last night to go to her room when I got up for a letter for Master Alick to take to town."

" And where is that letter?" asked Mrs. Dudley.

"On the hall table, ma'am, I believe. Miss Bessie left it there herself after she had wrote it."

"What made you lock the passage-door after you?"

" Miss Bessie told me to, ma'am."

Heather could not understand the matter at all. She did not believe that there was a sentence of truth in the girl's statement; but what her object might be in speaking falsely, she was unable to imagine.

" Miss Ormson is awake, then ?" she said, at length.

"Yes, ma'am—leastways she was when I saw her."

Without another word, Mrs. Dudley turned to regain the hall. She wanted to see if the letter were really on the slab, and then she meant to go to Bessie's room and ascertain whether or not Priscilla had spoken falsely.

The whole thing baffled Heather. But for the locking of the door, she should have thought nothing more about the matter; but what object either Bessie or Priscilla could have in thus cutting off immediate communication between the two parts of the house, she was quite unable to divine.

There on the slab lay Bessie's letter—a thick letter, for Heather lifted and held it in her hand for a moment; then she laid it down again, and ascended the front staircase, slowly and thoughtfully.

She had not reached the landing, however, before Priscilla was beside her.

"Ma'am—Mrs. Dudley," began the girl, " you can turn me out of the house this moment, if you like. I told you a lie about that letter. I did not go to Miss Bessie's room for it. Miss Bessie is gone."

"Gone!" Heather looked at the girl, and blankly repeated that word after her.

"Yes, ma'am; and there is a letter for you, please, on the toilet-table," at which point in her confession Prissy began to whimper.

"Don't do that," said Mrs. Dudley, almost angrily. "Go on before me to Miss Ormson's room, and be quiet."

Thus ordered, Priscilla walked along the passage, and, opening the door of Bessie's bedchamber, stood aside to allow Mrs. Dudley to enter.

Heather, as she did so, glanced hurriedly round the apartment. There was no disorder, no confusion; everything looked precisely as it might have done, had Bessie been there—only Bessie was not there.

Heather went up to the bed, and put her hand on the sheet. It felt warm, and she turned to Priscilla, saying, interrogatively—

"She has only just left the house?"

"She went at one o'clock, ma'am."

"Impossible! I have been in the room myself since four o'clock, and she was sleeping then."

"That was me, ma'am; and I was not asleep. I

heard you come in—I never went to sleep all night.
I'd have given anything, ma'am, if I might have
told you.　I never was so miserable in all my life—
and poor Miss Bessie, she were a-crying dreadful."

"Where is she gone?"

"I don't know, ma'am."

"Who is she gone with?"

"That gentleman as is so sweet on her."

"You don't mean Mr. Harcourt?"

"Lor'! no, ma'am; that other what she came back
from church to meet yesterday."

Utterly bewildered, Heather stood in the middle
of the room, confounded and almost stupified.

Had any one come to her and said Bessie was
dead, she could not have felt more shocked—more
grieved.　Under her eyes this thing had been going
on—this deception from day to day, and from week
to week—and she had never even suspected its
existence.　Her very servant had been cognisant
of it; this girl, this false, cheating, untruthful Prissy
Dobbin, had been persuaded by Bessie to conceal the
mischief until it was too late to repair it.　And
Bessie, too, that bright, gay, affectionate creature,
was but a hypocrite and a deceiver!　Mrs. Dudley

felt this to be the last drop in the cup, and, covering her face, wept bitterly.

"Don't 'ee, ma'am," implored Priscilla, "don't 'ee take on so ! Read what Miss Bessie says, mayhap that 'ill tell you where she's gone. The gentleman worships the very ground she treads on; and they would have told you, only something about his father, I don't rightly know what, prevented them. Miss Bessie prayed and begged him yesterday to let her speak to you. He wanted her, right or wrong, to go off with him then, but she wouldn't; she said she wouldn't spoil your Christmas Day, not for fifty husbands—she did."

"You were very fond of Miss Bessie?" Mrs. Dudley said, inquiringly.

"Main fond, ma'am," answered the girl. "I took to her from the day she talked to me in the field, and give I that harf a crown."

"Then don't go chattering about her having gone off with any one, Prissy. If you are fond of her, show your fondness by keeping silence."

And with that, Mrs. Dudley, first bidding Prissy stay with Lally, in case she wakened, went and roused her husband.

"Arthur," she said, "Bessie is off—she has eloped.   What are we to do?"

"Bessie eloped—Bessie off!   Heather, you must be dreaming!"

"I wish I were," answered his wife.   "Is there any use in trying to follow her, do you think?"

"There might be, if we knew where she was gone," Arthur replied.   "What does she say in her letter?" he added, noticing the paper in his wife's hand.

"She does not give a clue," said Heather.   "She merely states she is gone to be married, and that, whenever her husband allows her, she will write again."

"Better call up Alick," suggested Arthur; and, accordingly, Alick was called.

"They have four hours' start," said the young man, practically, when he had heard Heather's story, "and their plans must have been well laid.   I will follow if you like, but I think it is useless.   They are in London by this time."

"What makes you think they have gone to London?" asked Heather.

"Because it is the only place in which to be lost,"

answered the youth. And the three stood and looked at each other for a few moments in utter silence.

A great blow had suddenly fallen on them, and they felt stunned with its force.

That such a thing should have happened there! that they should all have bidden each other good-night, without a suspicion of coming evil—and that this should have come to pass before morning!

Heather was the first to speak.

"And Mr. Harcourt, too—what will he say?"

"If he be a wise man, 'that he is well rid of her,'" answered Arthur. "She must be a bad girl —a bad, false girl."

"But, oh! so good to Lally," said Heather, deprecatingly; "and I do not think it was of her own free will she went now—I do not—I believe she was driven to it. Read her letter, Arthur—read how she says she tried to like Mr. Harcourt, and how her mother forced her on. If I only knew she were married, I could rest satisfied."

And so husband and wife talked on, while Alick, standing by, remained resolutely silent.

He would tell nothing about it; he would say

nothing concerning the stranger they had met at North Kemms; he would not utterly destroy Heather's faith, and show her that Bessie had been a deceiver from the beginning. His heart was yearning after the girl, but he would not speak a word that could give a clue as to whom she had eloped with.

She had prayed him not to tell Heather, and he would be faithful to his trust. From him Heather never should know how false this girl had been— this girl with the lovely face, and the sweet, winning manners, which had gained her so many friends.

"The matter should be kept quiet;" each attributing different meanings to that expression, agreed as to the expediency of this course. Arthur said he would go to town with Alick, and take Bessie's letter on to her father.

"Then, Mr. Ormson can do whatever he thinks best," said the Squire; and Heather at once went to see that breakfast was got ready for the brothers before their departure.

"I wonder who the devil she can have picked up," remarked Squire Dudley, when his wife left the room; "you never saw anybody hanging about the place, did you, Alick?"

Very truthfully, Alick answered that he had not; but still in his own soul he felt satisfied Bessie had gone off with the stranger, who sat in the same pew with them, and restored Miss Ormson's prayer-book on that Sunday when he and his cousin walked across the fields to North Kemms church, talking as they went.

CHAPTER VIII.

MR. STEWART'S PROPOSAL.

THE woman who would rule her household well, had need to be endowed by Heaven with almost every virtue. She should be quick to perceive and slow to act; not given to rash judgments, nor easily moved to anger. She should be patient and long-suffering. She should remember that she is an absolute auto-crat in her small domain, and be merciful accord-ingly. Her servants are but after all as children, who have no claim to a parent's care and affection. She can take the bread out of their mouths, and, if they have been happy with her, drive them forth from Eden into the cold bleak world which is all before them; she can make or mar their futures; she can be lenient, or she can be harsh. She can be cruel—like the servant who, going out loosed from his lord's presence, seized upon his fellow-servant, crying, "Pay me that thou owest;" or she can have compassion on their infirmities, remembering that the God of the whole earth has had compassion on her.

She can be hard and exacting, demanding full measure and strict change; she can hold the scales steadily, and if there be a feather's weight too little, cast them out; or she may be merciful as her Father in Heaven is merciful, and be very patient towards those who try her patience, and her temper, and her Christianity daily. She can be the model, managing, worldly mistress, or she may be the mistress which the Lord shall approve when He cometh to His kingdom. She can resolve the whole question into one of work and wage, or she can go further, and strive so to rule herself, and those she has under her, that when the long account comes to be made up—that account between rich and poor, which will never be closed till eternity—the Great Judge shall say she has done her feeble best, that although only one talent was given unto her, it was not buried in the ground, but put out to usury, returning ample interest.

So far, this story has been written in vain, if any reader have failed to comprehend that Heather Dudley was one of those women, "the eyes of whose maidens turned unto her;" and it will, therefore, readily be conceived, that although many persons would have incontinently turned Priscilla Dobbin out of the house, and refused to sleep another night under the same roof with such a double-faced, artful little minx, Mrs. Dudley felt sorry for the girl and inclined to make allowances.

She had loved Bessie greatly, and she was but young. Her life was all before her, and Heather could not reconcile it to her conscience to mar it at the outset. She had her talk with the girl, during the course of which Prissy was, after the manner of her class, silent, and apparently sulky. Nevertheless, she departed from the audience-chamber red around the nose, watery about her eyes, and generally depressed in her spirits.

She had thought Miss Bessie's elopement a fine thing till "it came to the bit," thus she expressed herself; but when they mutually had that bit between their teeth she did not much relish the undertaking.

"She was to take me as her maid, mum," Priscilla informed Heather; "but he would not let her. He said she could send for me afterwards; but now, ma'am, if you'll let me stay with you, I would rather. I'll never even think about leaving you again."

This piece of information was imparted some weeks subsequently; during the course of those weeks, nothing had been heard of or from Bessie. Where she was gone, with whom she was gone off, remained as great enigmas to the family at the Hollow, as they did to her friends in town. From Priscilla, indeed, Heather gathered that the cavalier was tall, dark, handsome, and liberal; but this was but a poor clue with which to start on a search after Bessie, and so no one attempted to follow it.

She had chosen her own course, and her place knew her no more. All in vain, Heather looked for a letter each morning—no letter ever came. All in vain, Lally fretted after Bessie, and stretched out her arms for the pretty cousin who was gone no one knew where. Mr. Ormson advertised daily in the *Times* to B—ss—e O——n, without ever receiving a ghost of a reply. Mr. Harcourt paid "private inquiry fees," but still nothing came of all his searching. Mrs. Ormson, figuratively, washed her hands of Bessie, and scored her name out of the family Bible—a volume she never opened except upon high and rare occasions; the poor father watched his opportunity, and wrote the name in again, the first time Mrs. Ormson left her keys in the door of the cupboard where she kept this tell-tale volume of dates and ages. Dr. Marsden said he had always expected something of the kind, and Heather almost began to hate this strange man who came in as chorus to every misfortune of the family.

"I knew she never would marry Harcourt," affirmed this clever practitioner, the first time he and Mrs. Dudley met after the occurrence ; " the fellow must have been a fool to believe her."

"And why did you not think she would marry him ?" asked Heather, meekly.

"Oh ! her head was always running on a very different kind of husband to a struggling lawyer ; and I only hope it is a husband she has got, and not a lover, who will be packing her home to be a disgrace and burden to her family some of these fine days."

"I should not think Bessie very likely to return

to her family, whether she be married or not," Heather answered, a little bitterly. She could not help being a trifle short with Dr. Marsden, whose first-born was still at Berrie Down, a very thorn in the flesh of every member composing the household.

Never out of mischief, never still, always teasing, eternally prying about, listening and meddling, even Heather at last declared, if she only had the money to spare, she would rather pay for Harry's education than be tormented with him.

But there was an end coming to all such torments and discomforts—an end which found Heather but poorly prepared for its advent; and the beginning of this end was a visit Arthur received on the 2nd of January, from a tall, thin, grey-haired, hard-featured individual, who sent in his card as—

" Mr. Allan Stewart."

" Being at Kemms Park," he stated, after the first civilities had been gone through, " I thought you would excuse my calling, and talking over a little matter of business with you. It is about that house in Lincoln's Inn Fields; you know, Mr. Dudley, we cannot purchase it from you. I am very sorry indeed, but such a thing is quite out of the question."

"Why?" Arthur demanded.

"Well, in the first place, the position is anything but desirable; and, in the second, the price you ask is prohibitory. Besides, what do we want with purchasing properties? we need only rent offices. It would be the merest waste of money for us to do otherwise."

"Mr. Black assured me there was not the slightest doubt of the Company purchasing my lease," answered Squire Dudley.

"Yes, because Mr. Black thought the management was going to be left entirely to him," was the reply. "Mr. Black now finds he was a little mistaken, and that, being mistaken, he led you astray."

"He was the originator of the Company, or else I have been greatly misinformed," said Arthur, defiantly.

"You have not been misinformed," Mr. Stewart answered; "but the originator of a company does not necessarily mean the proprietor."

Squire Dudley remained silent, digesting this piece of knowledge, while Mr. Stewart proceeded—

"We directors are not necessarily his puppets because he brought us together. Although he obtained our names, and qualified us to act on the board, he did not thereby obtain dominion over us, body and soul for ever. Evidently, Mr. Dudley, you are not a man of business, and you do not understand much about commercial matters—indeed, Mr. Black implied that fact to me; therefore, as I happened to be staying with Miss Baldwin, I thought I would walk over, and have a little friendly conversation with you."

"Do you mean," asked Mr. Dudley, harking back to the original question, "that you absolutely refuse to purchase these premises in Lincoln's Inn Fields?"

"That is my meaning," was the reply; "if you press the matter, of course it will be brought before the board, Mr. Black, probably, acting as your mouthpiece; but if you take my advice, you will not press the point, nor have it brought before the board; for I tell you fairly, the line must be drawn somewhere, and at that point I mean it to be marked broadly."

"You are not the proprietor of the Company, are you?" asked Arthur.

"No; but I am the largest shareholder and the most influential man on the board," was the reply.

"And what do you think of the scheme?" inquired Arthur, eagerly.

"I think the scheme a good one, if it be not swamped; if the capital be not all jobbed away on such purchases, for instance, as this house of yours."

"Do you imply that I——," began the Squire; but Mr. Stewart cut across his sentence with—

"I imply nothing; all I would suggest is, that as at Mr. Black's instance you bought a very bad bargain, you should not seek to foist that bargain at a profit on your own Company, but wait patiently for dividends, and be thankful for any profit on your shares the Lord may in due time send you."

"Do you know, sir," asked Arthur, "that my money has advertised this Company?'

"Black said something of the kind," answered Mr. Stewart; "and what he said, I am very sorry to hear confirmed by you."

"I have sold my crops, I have sold my stock, I have accepted bills, all on the faith of making my fortune out of this bread affair. Mr. Black declared I could get my money back three times over by buying from time to time such properties as he might advise—shops, mills, and so forth. He assured me he could and would guarantee the Company purchasing them from me on the most favourable terms. He mentioned to me the names of several individuals who have all made large fortunes in the same way."

" Yes, I know many men, as you say, who have obtained their money by jobbing," was the calm answer ; " but they should not have got fat so soon had I been on the direction."

" It is rather hard upon me, though, to be made your scapegoat," said Arthur.

" Perhaps so," agreed Mr. Stewart; " but you know the innocent often suffer for the guilty. In fact, the scapegoat of which you have just spoken had not, so far as I am aware, committed any sin that should have doomed him to go unto a land not inhabited. He was selected impartially by lot, and then had to bear the iniquities of the children of Israel. You, Mr. Dudley, are chosen by accident to bear by proxy Mr. Black's sins of over·appropriation. He has already had quite as many pickings for himself as any company can bear, and we cannot now tolerate his beginning to pick for his friends."

"And your object in coming to tell me all this, Mr. Stewart?" demanded Arthur.

"Come, he is not quite an idiot," reflected that gentleman, while he answered aloud—"My object is *bona fide;* I want to benefit you and myself also. I wish to explain exactly what I will and what I will not do. To begin with the last. I will not agree to the purchase of those premises in Lincoln's Inn, but I shall not oppose the Company renting them from year to year ; and, if you like to resign your directorship, I will see that you are appointed secretary at a commencing salary of one thousand pounds per annum.

"What has the secretary to do?" asked Arthur.

"Very little, except remain honest," was the reply.

"And why do you wish me to be secretary?" he further demanded.

"Because I think we may depend upon you; because I know we could not depend on the secretary nominated by Mr. Black. In matters of this kind it does not do to stand too much upon cere-mony. Am I wrong, Mr. Dudley, in supposing a thousand a year would prove an agreeable addition to your income ?"

"I am not aware, sir," answered Arthur, in a moment all in a flame with anger, "that I have, in the course of our conversation, led you to believe I am short of money."

"There is a difference between being short of money and desiring more money," answered Mr. Stewart, calmly. "I concluded that, if you were a perfectly satisfied man, you would have rested con-tent among your herds and flocks, and not sought to increase your store in the City. I thought I would come and talk this affair over with you before our next meeting ; but if my doing so has assumed the character of an intrusion, I can only apologise and withdraw."

Having concluded which speech, Mr. Stewart rose from his chair, and, bowing to Arthur, would have left the room, had his host not entreated him to remain.

"I am almost mad, I think," said the Squire, putting his hand to his forehead. " Excuse me if I seemed rude. I do not believe I knew what I was saying. It is a desperate experiment, Mr. Stewart, for a man who knows nothing whatever of business to allow himself to be drawn into it."

" Yes," answered the director, coolly ; " and it is in the interests of such men that I decline permitting this Company to be made a job, for the advancement and enriching of the few at the expense of the many. In my opinion, you have acted foolishly in advancing large sums of money to Mr. Black ; but it is to Mr. Black you should look for repayment, not to the shareholders."

Arthur made no reply. He sat with his head bent forward thinking to himself, "what a cursed idiot I have been !" This was the first check he had met with, and he bore it with proportionate impatience. When a man has grown used to disappointment and reverses ; when he has met with a long series of losses and failures ; when his temper has become, after a fashion, macadamized, and his spirit broken under the wheels of constantly passing hearses containing the bodies of his hopes, his certainties, his ambitious aspirings ; then the sharp pang which was once so impossible to endure, is dulled to a kind of quiet aching. The pain wears itself out as the months and the years go by; and he who once chafed, grows apathetic; and she who formerly wept, now smiles and bears in silence.

But Arthur Dudley's pain was fresh, and it had, moreover, come sharply and suddenly upon him.

He had been stricken unprepared, and, though the wound inflicted might not be very severe, still it smarted as much as though his life had been placed in jeopardy.

All this Mr. Stewart observed and noted.

"That man has (for him) played high," he thought, "and staked not merely money but hope on the game;" then finding Arthur still resolutely kept silence, he proceeded:

"Mr. Black will altogether make a handsome thing out of this Company."

"Yes, and he promised to go halves with me!" interrupted Arthur, hoarsely.

"Indeed! and now he would fulfil that promise by showing you what to buy, and then recommending us to purchase from you; a very nice way of doing business for him, doubtless—very nice indeed."

"I wish to God I had never gone into the Company at all!" broke out the Squire, weakly and passionately; "and I did it on the strength of your name, and the names of men like you."

"That was foolish," said Mr. Stewart; "if you had asked me for advice, I should decidedly have recommended you to leave the Protector Flour and Bread Company, Limited, alone."

"But you expect to make money out of it," said Arthur, obstinately.

"Yes, but I am also prepared to lose money," was the reply; "which fact constitutes the difference between us. If a man be, as I have always been, a speculator, he takes the rough with the smooth, the failure with the success. I lay out my plans as well as I can, but I, at the same time, take my chance. Moreover, Mr. Dudley, I can afford to wait for success; you, perhaps, are not quite so fortunately situated."

"Did you come here to insult me?" asked the Squire.

"No; on the contrary, I came here to help you, if you will permit me to do so. We are not playing quite a fair game," added the director, with sudden frankness. "You are showing me your hand—I have scarcely given you a sight of mine. Suppose, I say unreservedly, I also have embarked more money in this venture than I should care to lose, we should then stand on more equal terms. You have advanced money to float the Company; I am a shareholder—a *bona-fide* shareholder, remember—to a large amount; I do not want our ship to go to the bottom, neither do you; Mr. Black, a very worthy individual, no doubt, has a knack of floating companies, and then sinking them. Now, it is not your interest, any more than it is mine, that this Company should fail; we want to see the shares at a premium, and to secure regularly-paid and satisfactory dividends. There is nothing to prevent such a desirable consummation, if the affairs of the Company be only properly managed. Now, if any nominee of your friend, Mr. Black, be appointed permanent secretary, there is no telling what the end of the matter may prove. Therefore, I offer you this secretaryship; say the word, and you shall have it. We will rent the Lincoln's Inn premises from you; there is a good house there in which you might reside, and you would then be on the spot to look after your own interests, and those of your fellow-shareholders."

Arthur wavered: the temptation was great, the salary sounded large, but he did not feel inclined so readily to turn his back on an old friend.

"If you had such an opinion of Mr. Black," he said, "why did you ever go into this Company with him?"

"As for that," answered Mr. Stewart, with a smile, "there is scarcely an undertaking of the kind which has not one black sheep at least in its ranks. Now, I am quite aware of the nature of Mr. Black's weakness, and, you may recollect, it is stated to be better to have to do with a devil you know, than a devil you do not know. Further, Mr. Black is undeniably clever, and he has, equally undeniably, got hold of a good thing."

"And yet you say, had I consulted you in the first instance, you would have advised me to keep clear of it!"

"On the terms—yes," was Mr. Stewart's reply. "Had Mr. Black come to you and said, 'Here are a couple of hundred shares, paid up, which will qualify you to act as a director, let me have your

name on our board in exchange,' I should have recommended you to accept his offer, because, if the
Company succeeded, there were the shares; if it
failed, you had no liability; either way, you would
have been safe. But when it comes to advancing
money—even on the best security that Mr. Black
could offer—the case is materially altered. I should
not have counselled such a risk as that, Mr. Dudley,
depend upon it!"

"Do you think Mr. Black will not repay me,
then?" asked Arthur.

"I do not think Mr. Black can repay you,"
amended Mr. Stewart; "with the best will in the
world, I am confident that he has not the means
of doing so at present. His other companies will
swallow up every available sixpence he can scrape
together for the next twelvemonth."

"But I have my shares," said the Squire.

"True; but paid-up shares are never of any
real marketable value, unless all the shares are
paid up."

"Why?" was the next inquiry.

"Because," explained Mr. Stewart, "no man will
pay ten pounds for that which he can buy imme-

diately for two : as, for instance, if you went on the market to-morrow, you would not be so foolish as to purchase a paid-up share, in any company, for twenty pounds, if you could procure exactly the same advantages for five. You could but pay your calls, if they were demanded ; you would not rush to your bankers and write a cheque for the full sum at once. In some prospectuses—in one of Mr. Black's, by-the-bye—there is a very delicious paragraph, to the effect, that 'although no further calls will be made at shorter intervals than three months, and then in amounts not exceeding one pound per share, still the shareholders may, at any time after allotment, pay up their shares in full, receiving interest on such payments at the rate of six per cent. per annum!' I never met with a man desirous of paying up his shares in full, however," finished Mr. Stewart with a quiet laugh.

"Do you mean, then, to tell me that until all the shares are paid up, those I have will remain valueless ?" demanded Arthur.

" Comparatively so," was the reply.

" Then what good—if I cannot sell my shares, nor dispose of my property, and if there be no chance of Mr. Black dividing his profits with me—is this Company likely to do to me or mine?"

"You will have your dividends, if we are lucky enough ever to get any," answered Mr. Stewart; "and, should you entertain my proposal, I promise you the secretaryship also; that will yield you a thousand a year. Perhaps you will consider the matter, Mr. Dudley, and let me know your decision before Saturday next. You have my address. I shall be returning to town to-morrow."

And the great man rose to go, having, as he felt confident, settled the business which had brought him down into Hertfordshire.

Arthur accompanied him to the outer door.

"What a lovely place you have!" said the director, looking round, approvingly. "A spot I should covet, if it were twenty miles nearer London."

"It is very inaccessible," Arthur agreed. This light kind of conversation appeared to him very much like the political small talk to which a surgeon will sometimes treat a patient next day after an operation.

"It would not be exactly convenient for a man who wished to be in town every day at eight o'clock," suggested Mr. Stewart; "but it is very charming, nevertheless. Good-morning!" And this man, who was between seventy and eighty years of age, started off to walk back to Kemms Park, as briskly as Arthur himself might have done.

"Old enough to have given up grubbing after money," muttered Arthur, criticizing his visitor's retreating figure; as though a man ever fancied himself old enough to relinquish the occupation of his life, so long as he could hold a pen or dictate a letter, bring a bill into Parliament, or buy to advantage on the Stock Exchange.

Old enough! Is it not only the young, now-a-days, who feel old and cry aloud for rest; who grow weary and tired of the heat and burden of the noon-tide? When the back has become used to the pack, and the world's collar has ceased to gall, the horse, let it be ever so old, will amble along the familiar road, without whip or spur to urge him on. It is the colts who turn aside, who long for the idle days and the green pastures, for the meadows where the holiday-folks are making merry, and the silvery streams flowing through the midst.

CHAPTER IX.

A FEW BILLS.

HITHERTO, Squire Dudley had, since his connection with Mr. Black, experienced no shortness of money. The man who spends two years' income in one, does not, as a rule, find the pecuniary shoe begin to pinch until he enters on the second twelvemonth, and realises to himself the truth that it is impossible both to spend and to have.

There is a time of plenty during which the prodigal wastes his substance and takes life easily, and then after that comes the season of famine, when he is fain to content himself with very roots and husks—when, having once entertained like a prince, he is compelled to expiate his folly in retirement, and refresh his spirit with herbs of the field, and water from the brook.

In Joseph's dream, the seven fat kine preceded the seven lean; the same rule was observed also in Squire Dudley's less prudent experience, though it produced by no means a like result. Never, for many and many a long year, had Arthur been so flush of cash, and so careless about expending it, as in the days before Mr. Stewart's friendly visit.

Lightly come, lightly gone, that was the way with his money then! It is difficult for a man, such as Arthur Dudley, exactly to realise the fact that lending his name may eventually prove the hardest day's work he ever did in his life; in truth, it is a fact difficult for any one unacquainted with business, to understand theoretically. It is but a few strokes of the pen, aud the thing is done. Your obliging friend, who has been kind enough to draw out the document for you, and perhaps even buy the stamp, gets the paper discounted. He takes out of it what you promised to let him have, and duly hands over the remainder.

The money is then a certainty—the bill, an illusion, is gone; your friend will meet it, never fear. He tells you not to trouble your head about the matter. Like Mr. Black, he will " take a memorandum of it," and that memorandum seems to you a perfect security for the genuineness of the transaction.

Time, however, goes by; the money is spent, the bill is coming due; then it is the first item which appears the illusion; the latter, the certainty. Concerning wasted sovereigns and mis-spent five-pound notes, a useless jeremiade is sung.

If you had but the past to live over again, you think, how differently you would act; meantime, however, you cannot live the past over again, and the bill is coming due.

When it does come due, there is only one thing of which you may be morally certain, namely, that you will have to take it up; that, spite of your friend's memorandum and assurances, he will be at the last moment disappointed, and so disappoint you.

You have had your cake, or at least a portion of that dainty; you have eaten and digested it; and now comes the time for payment; now come the anxious days and sleepless nights; now begins the begging, borrowing, realising; you have within five pounds of the amount required—you might as well not have a penny; you must scrape those other hundred shillings together before five o'clock on the evening of the day of presentation, or else your precious document falls into the notary's hands. In his hands there is still another short chance for your credit; but fail to avail yourself of that, and what ensues?

Mr. Black was the man to have given every possible information on this subject. I do not think any other human being ever had so many bills returned to him as he; it is doubtful if any one in the length and breadth of London had devoted so much time to raising the wind; whether there ever existed any one who, so almost invariably, never took up his bills at all, or drove up with what he called the needful to the door of his bank, at the very stroke almost of four, or rushed away to the other bank where the bill was lying, or else to the notary's in Finch Lane.

What a reality dishonoured bills may prove, Mr. Peter Black had, many a time and oft, personally tested, in the pleasant retirement of the Cripplegate Hotel.

In the lofty public room of that desirable house

of public entertainment, he had frequently made vows against paper, and mentally signed the pledge of total abstinence against all accommodation bills, but vows registered among a number of fellow-victims, amid a Babel of strange tongues, or in the shady courts and cool corridors that used to be so much approved and patronized by former dwellers in Whitecross Street; with visions of angry creditors, and an unsympathetic commissioner in perspective, are apt to be forgotten when the man is free again —free to push his way forward—to trade, and struggle, and strive, and get into trouble again, if he list.

A bill was nothing to Mr. Black. He had done in bills all his life. Trading, as was his fashion, always in advance of his fortune, it will readily be believed that " paper" was to him the very soul of business—that soul, in fact, which animated what would otherwise have been a very dead, stupid, helpless sort of body.

Mr. Black's diary of bills to meet was a literary curiosity well worth inspecting, if it were borne at the same time in mind that the promoter had not sixpenny-worth of real tangible property in the world.

But he had that which often stands a man in much better stead than property: he had faith; and it is not in religious matters only that faith is able to remove mountains.

He believed utterly in himself and in his own financial abilities; by means of this belief, he was enabled not merely to remove mountains, but also to create them out of molehills; wonderful companies—endless Limited Liabilities—great works were developed from the merest, paltriest, smallest businesses that any one could mention.

And because of his faith he was, conversationally, rather a pleasant man with whom to be connected in business. Let who else would, sing a poor song, he "never said die;" let who might be cross and changeable, faint-hearted and desponding, Mr. Black was always the same.

Always self-reliant, cheery, hopeful, certain of success, that sort of man who never meets an acquaintance with a long face; who is not affected by the weather, who shakes hands just as hearti y if the rain be pouring down Heavens hard, as he would if it were the finest day in summer; who considers snow a joke, and frost an agreeable change; who is never down on his luck; whose barometer, according to his own showing, is always rising; with whom it is, at least, fair weather from January till December; who, if he do chance to get a heavy blow, is only staggered by it for the moment; who is not eternally complaining about his own health, or his wife's health, or the sickness of his ten children, or the bad state of trade, or the difficulties of fighting through, but who always says, with a cheery nod—

"Quite well, thank you. Business? oh, capital; never had such a month—more work to do than I can get through. Wish I could cut myself up to be in a dozen places at once. All well with you? that's right; good-day, good-day!"

To a man like this, it may readily be imagined, Arthur Dudley proved a perfect mine of wealth—a true God-send, as he reverently remarked to Mr. Bailey Crossenham.

When first he and Arthur started together in the new Company, Mr. Black informed the Brothers Crossenham that "he drew it mild with the Squire;" but soon, finding that gentleman believed every word he told him, the promoter grew less delicate, and would persuade his kinsman to accept three or four bills for him in the course of a week.

It was such a rare experience for Mr. Black to hold thoroughly good paper — paper concerning which no objection could be made, that he felt it would be quite a slighting of Providence not to enjoy that strange sensation thoroughly.

To allow a name like Dudley's to waste its sweetness among the Hertfordshire fields, and never figure on stamped slips of foolscap in banks and discount offices, would have seemed to Mr. Black the merest quixotism.

Here was what he had always sighed for—a good name. Like the individual who would have given ten thousand pounds for a good character, because, on the strength of that character, he could have trebled that sum immediately, Mr. Black conceived that one good name must inevitably lead to more. Should he suffer this gift to lie unused—should he allow this talent to remain buried in a napkin? Never; a thousand times, never. And, accordingly, he employed Arthur's name as freely as he might his own, which is saying a good deal; and Arthur rested satisfied.

Would not money turn in after Christmas. Were he and Mr. Black not to go shares? Would those thousands not be returning to him from the sale of the Lincoln's Inn property? Was the Company not well thought of—well talked about? Had not Walter Hope—spite of his aunt's remonstrances—added his name to the Direction, without a moment's hesitation? Had he not said to Mrs. Walter Hope,—

"And the dividends shall be. yours, my love?" an arrangement which met with that lady's entire approval. Had Mr. Douglas Croft not remarked that Black was " a sly fox, but a devilish clever fellow—a fellow who could float anything, if he only took it into his head to do so?" Had he not tasted of the sweets of spending money freely—of spending without pausing first to consider, "Can I afford this expense?"

His deeds now went in front, and his prudent thoughts lagged slowly behind. After the long Lent of fasting and humiliation—of poverty and strict abstinence from all extravagance—from all worldly pleasures—all social amusements—there suddenly dawned an Easter morning on his life, full of brightness and pleasure—a morning when the old traditions were forgotten, and a new era was begun.

Mr. Stewart's visit was the first occurrence which cast an actual shadow over all this radiancy. Previously, light clouds might have swept across the sky—a few misgivings through his heart—so far, he had neither seen nor heard anything of the money, some portion of which he knew, for certain, Mr. Black must have received. Neither had letters from that gentleman arrived with quite their accustomed punctuality at Berrie Down. "Christmas-time," the promoter stated, threw everything, for a short period, out of gear, and then ensued silence, until on the morning of Mr. Stewart's visit came a communication ending with these ominous words,—

"I am right for the bill due on Saturday, but should like to see you about the others."

About the others! Good Heavens, what concern were they of Squire Dudley's? Mr. Black, or the bank, or the Company, or somebody, was to take them up; certainly not Arthur.

The herds and flocks, the crops and Nellie, had represented to Squire Dudley tangible property advanced into the "Protector Bread and Flour Company, Limited," but his name seemed the very vaguest valuable possible, and he had stared at first, when Mr. Black suggested using it.

Now, however, the very vagueness of the threatened peril filled his mind with alarm. What could Mr. Black want with him? and what did he mean by being "right for that on Saturday?" Was he not right for all? and if he were not, how did he expect the sight of Squire Dudley to put him so?

There was a terrible uncertainty about the matter which seemed very frightful to Arthur; and then, on the top of this letter—following it almost as swiftly as the thunderclap does lightning—came Mr. Stewart, and the interview already detailed.

Altogether, the second day in the new year was not one marked with a white stone in Squire Dudley's memory, yet it brought, in due time, its consolation, for pondering over the matter, Arthur discovered two tangible pieces of comfort on which to hang his hopes: one, the offer of the secretary-ship; the other, Mr. Stewart's own evident belief in the ultimate success of the Company.

"So I will run up to town to-morrow and see Black," decided Squire Dudley—who had vainly striven to catch a glimpse of that gentleman on Boxing Day, when he went to inform Mr. Ormson of his daughter's misdemeanor—"and I will tell him frankly about the secretaryship, so that there may be no underhand dealing in the matter, and I can see how the place in Lincoln's Inn would suit for a residence, and then give Mr. Stewart a decided answer."

Already his opera-box and horses and carriages, his grand town residence, his hunters, his hacks, his fashionable friends, were dwindling down to a thousand a year and a free house—to work which, slight though it might be, was more than he had ever thought of previously attempting. Already the dream-castle was beginning to fade away, and the sober stone-and-mortar building of reality taking its place; but Arthur Dudley resolutely refused to see the inevitable change which had commenced being wrought.

Bitten by the mania prevalent amongst those men with whom he had latterly freely associated, the Squire would not regard the secretaryship as any thing except a useful step onward—a mere trifle which would keep him in funds till the Company began to pay dividends, and shares rose to some enormous premium.

When a person is making an imaginative fortune, there can be no possible reason why he should not do the thing thoroughly.

Mentally, it is as easy to nett fifty thousand pounds as one—to send shares up to fabulous prices as to keep them at par; in fact, if a man once lets his fancy get the reins, he may mount to whatever height pleases him and his charioteer best.

The only drawback to which proceeding is, that if he get a fall, he stands a chance of being badly injured by it. Even Fancy seldom travels with a free ticket—there are expenses incident on a too great intimacy with that fair lady. She is apt to lead people a good deal astray sometimes, with her glancing smiles and her bright bewitching eyes— with her sweet tones, which fall so pleasantly on the ear—with her seductive words, which ring such pleasant changes on the usually prosaic bells of life.

But Arthur Dudley was not a man to turn back into the cold realms of reality when once he had basked in the sunshine of prospective success. Children think that they can keep back the rain-cloud by turning their eyes away from that corner of the heavens whence the wind is blowing; and, in like manner, Squire Dudley persisted in looking at the spot of blue which revealed itself in his sky, and resolutely ignoring all the blackness which was sweeping up behind.

"The 'Protector' should pay"—even Mr. Stewart had said something to that effect; and the very first thing which met Arthur's delighted gaze, as he walked down Gray's Inn Lane from the King's Cross Station, was a huge vehicle—apparently constructed on the joint models of a police-van and a cattle-truck, driven by a man in a quiet livery of orange and green, and guarded by a hanging footman, decked out in the like complimentary colours —which vehicle bore on its sides this inscription:—

"VIS UNITA FORTIOR,"

the motto of the Company, its device being a bundle of sticks firmly tied together.

Then followed—

"PROTECTOR"

FLOUR AND BREAD COMPANY (LIMITED).

INCORPORATED UNDER ACT OF PARLIAMENT,

For the purpose of Supplying the Public with the Best Bread at the Lowest Possible Price.

If this did not look like business, Arthur wondered what would. If all that varnish and gilding, all that lettering and painting, did not indicate success, he was very much out in his calculations. It was only the third day for the vans to be out, and they had not yet lost their pristine brilliancy. They were clean and fresh, as though they had that moment come out of the builder's hands—the liveries were free from spot or stain—the brass of the harness was bright as lacquer—the horses were groomed to perfection—the drivers and the men behind both looked, in their fine conspicuous clothing, conscious and conceited, and, perhaps, a little shamefaced besides.

The London boys cheered the splendid convey-

ance, and put, at the same time, various rude questions to the individuals in charge.

The idle, dirty, half-starved looking women who
are always gathered round the entrance to those
wretched courts leading out of Gray's Inn Lane,
stared after the vehicle, and made audible comments
upon it, which Arthur could hear as he passed by.

Very well-dressed people also took notice of the
van, and wondered what the meaning of the motto
might be. Ladies were especially interested in this
question; and Arthur longed to stop and tell a few
of the sweet creatures—not merely the English of
Vis Unita Fortior, but also that he was one of the
directors in the great Company.

Walking down Gray's Inn Lane, the Squire certainly was a proof of the truth of his own quotation.
As a master baker, singly, he would have felt very
much ashamed of his trade, and vexed by any public
recognition of it. As a master baker, associated
with other gentlemen and noblemen also bakers,
Squire Dudley conceived himself a person of importance, one of a body of philanthropists, who, "hearing the cry of the people for bread, pure bread,
sweet, wholesome, nutritious bread, at a moderate

price, had determined on forming themselves into a Company which, under the name of the 'Protector,' should guard alike the rights of producer and consumer—supply the public with the best bread at the lowest remunerative prices—ensure to the shareholders a fair and certain return for capital—do away with unwholesome, ill-ventilated, badly-constructed, insufficient and uncleanly bakehouses, and render the trade wholesome and remunerative to the employés connected with it, instead of permitting it to remain, as hitherto, a blot on nineteenth century civilization—one of the most enervating, pestiferous, dangerous trades which could be conceived."—*Vide* Prospectus.

This is one of the many beauties of a Limited Liability Company : a man can have all the excitement, profit, and pleasure of trade, without any of its unpleasantness.

If he be one of the directors on the board of, say "The Private Dwelling Chimney-Sweeping Association," he still remains a gentleman.

In the Bankruptcy Court, indeed, where some singular anomalies are still permitted to exist, he might be styled a dealer and chapman ; but in West

End drawing-rooms his standing is above suspicion. He is a wise individual who, despising trade, is still not above making use of it; who, knowing nothing of business, would nevertheless go and reap of the corn which his hand neither planted nor watered; he can do, as Squire Dudley wished to do, " gather where he has not strawed," and march in and out of City offices as though the whole of the Lord Mayor's kingdom from Ludgate to the Tower, and from Moorgate to London Bridge, belonged to him.

It was with this feeling Arthur Dudley, spite of his anxieties, entered the temporary offices in Dowgate Hill, where he was greeted by Mr. Black with an uproarious joviality.

" Well, old fellow, and how are you? Bills brought you up express, I see; thought nothing short of them could get me a speedy sight of you. I did not want you about them at all, you know, really, for I could have sent you the renewals to sign by post as easily as not. Yes, we must renew. I have such a devil of a lot of things on hand at the present time—good things, but still all crying out for money. Well, and how are you? and your charming lady, and my friend Lally, you know? Poor little cricket! I

was deucedly sorry to hear of her being so ill ; and
oh ! isn't that a business about Ormson's daughter !
By Jove ! the old man is cut up, and no mistake.
Mrs. O. takes it better than he—comes the Roman
matron and that sort of thing; think I liked her
quite as well before I heard her declaiming against
the girl.   Mrs. Black believes her sister forced
Bessie to accept Harcourt against her will, and led
her a nice life at home over it.   I always considered
Mrs. O. a very superior sort of woman; but I
suppose God who made it is the only one who
rightly understands female nature.   It is an enigma
to me.   Who's she off with, Squire ?   Come, it is
all in the family, and you need not keep the matter
dark here."

"I have not the remotest idea," answered Arthur.
"No one seems able to give the slightest clue.   She
must have been a sly, deep girl to make a flight
like that.   She bribed one of the servants, went
down the back staircase, out across the farmyard,
away along the field avenue, and so into Berrie
Down Lane, where her lover, it appears, was
waiting for her."

"She was a very pretty girl, Dudley," said Mr.

Black, meditatively, speaking of her beauty already in the past tense.

"I never saw anything so particularly wonderful about her," answered Arthur, coolly.

"Well, she might not be your style, you know; but still she was undeniably pretty. Talking about style, by-the-bye, I saw your old flame, Mrs. Croft, yesterday. I suppose you are not touchy about a fellow speaking his mind concerning her? You had a miss there—such as a man might have of losing his life. I'd as lief be married to the devil. Croft asked me up to dinner, and I don't think that madame liked it; at any rate, she made herself so confoundedly disagreeable that Croft seemed downright ashamed of her. And didn't she nag him! that is enough. He broke a vase on the drawing-room chimney-piece after dinner, and I never heard a poor beast so pitched into in all my .ife. And before the servants, too! If she had said the one-half to me she said to him, I should not have minded doing six months for what I would have given her. A man was telling me a good thing about Croft the other day. It appears he had been complaining to some of his wife's male relations about the way she goes on, and this fellow, some fool of a swell, did not seem able to make out what exact fault Croft laid to her charge. ' Isn't she pwoper ?' he drawled out. ' Proper !' says Croft, in that sharp off-hand way of his, 'damnably proper.' Ah, we may laugh at it," went on Mr. Black, doubtless speaking figuratively, for he was not laughing, and not a ghost of a smile could have been detected on Arthur's face; " but it must be the very deuce to be tied to a woman like that. While she was going on at him, blowing him up sky-high, and sweeping about in her grand dress, with a crinoline big enough to have camped out under, I thought of your wife, Squire, and I said to a man this very morning, not half-an-hour ago,—

" Well, Dudley must be a deuced lucky fellow— not merely to have missed that woman, but to have got the wife he has. There is no sham there—no angel one day, and devil the next."

Arthur cleared his throat. He felt as though he were choking; he wanted to make some withering speech in answer to this officious fool, but he was not quick of wit nor ready with repartee.

First, to lose a woman, to be jilted, to have an

heiress slip out of his fingers, to be supplanted by a wealthier suitor, to be flung back from the height of prospective affluence to the dead level of certain poverty, and then to be congratulated on the subject, and called a lucky fellow! To hear another man who had gained the prize pitied for his success, and he, Arthur, felicitated on having chosen a wife who did not suit him in the least. Arthur knew Heather did not suit him—that she was not the woman he ought to have married. At that moment he felt very ungrateful both towards Heaven and the helpmeet Heaven had sent him, and he felt further that he hated Mr. Black with a perfect hatred, for which reason, as he could not think of any specially clever or cutting remark that might advantageously be uttered, he turned the conversation into a channel which he thought must prove disagreeable to Mr. Black, and said,—

"Speaking of Croft, Stewart called on me yesterday."

" Ah, yes,". answered the promoter, briskly; " been down staying with his cousin, the Honourable Augusta, I hear. That would be a nice suitable match, now; thought it likely he might call. He told you he meant to oppose the purchase of your Lincoln's Inn speculation, I suppose?"

"Your Lincoln's Inn speculation, rather," retorted Arthur, a little indignantly.

"*Our* Lincoln's Inn speculation, then, to meet the views of both parties," proposed Mr. Black. "So he called to tell you about that, did he? People's ideas of civility differ. I would just as soon call on a man to pick his pocket as to inform him I meant to overthrow his plans."

"That was not Mr. Stewart's sole object in calling," remarked Arthur.

"Oh! indeed; and what might his object be, if I am not too inquisitive?"

"Not at all; I came up partly on purpose to tell you. Guess the nature of the proposal he made."

"That you should wind up the Company, or try to do so; that he and you and Mr. Raidsford and Lord Kemms should start an opposition bakery of your own; that you should purchase Mr. Scrotter's flour-mill, and sell it to the Company; that you and Mr. Stewart should agree to support each other through everything. There, I have guessed often enough. What is this wonderful proposal which he made to you yesterday?"

"Guess again.   I would rather that you jumped at it yourself."

"Hang it! I can't guess what the old humbug wanted with you.   Did he propose marrying one of your sisters?—or——I have it!" exclaimed Mr Black; "he offered you the secretaryship?"

"He did."

"And you accepted it?"

"No, I did not: I felt a delicacy——"

"Felt nonsense!" interrupted Mr. Black; "how could you be such a simpleton? You must be rich to throw away a thousand a year for delicacy! Deuce a thing to do except sit before the fire for a certain number of hours reading the *Times*—have clerks under you to do everything—read the *Times* for you, if you like!   And a secretaryship to which you are appointed through the interest of Allan Stewart! By Jove! it is as good as an annuity. You felt a delicacy about interfering with Mr. Crossenham— that's the hitch, is it? Very nice, and proper, and gentlemanly indeed—very; but Crossenham, you see, is not going to retain the secretaryship—no, not if we went down on our knees and prayed him to keep it, which I, for one, have no intention of doing."

" Why will he not keep it?" asked Arthur, in amazement.

" Because it don't suit him," was the reply. " He has always been used to work, and he don't like idling. He says he has no fancy for loafing about, with his hands in his pockets, drawing only a poor two hundred and fifty a quarter, when there are thousands of pounds to be picked up by any one willing to look out for chances. Of course, he is quite another style of fellow from what you are, Dudley. He has been in business all his life ; and what really is a very good appointment for you, seems almost like shelving him. I thought, as his health was not very good, he might be glad of such a berth. But no ; he is hungering and thirsting after work—work, and no gammon—that is what he calls it. Besides, he hates talking to those swells who are quite in your way, you know. If Crossenham be your only objection, here is pen, ink, and paper— write at once to Mr. Stewart, and say you accept his offer."

" But if I do that, I bind myself not to ask the Company to purchase my Lincoln's Inn property."

" And much good it would do if you did ask the

Company to purchase it, with Allan Stewart against you! Look here, Dudley. Stewart is going to be the god of our board; so your best plan, if you want things to go pretty square, is, thankfully to receive all he likes to offer you. My power is gone, you know. Whenever he came crowing it over me, with his shares, and his influence, and his wealth, and his connection, I gave in at once; so take a friend's advice, and accept. Did he promise to rent the house from you? That is right. He proposed you should live there! The very best thing possible. Good airy rooms, central situation, near the theatres, accessible to everywhere!"

"And about those bills, Mr. Black?"

"Yes, about those bills! We must renew for a few months, till my ventures begin to make me some return. A mere matter of form! I will pay the interest, of course, and you shall have back the old bills. Here, Collins," cried Mr. Black, opening the door between the two offices, "run over the way and get me a pound's worth of bill-stamps. Three shilling and two shilling — four of each. Look sharp now, and don't be the whole day about it. While we are 'melting,' you might as well have a few hundreds, might you not, Dudley? You will want some money to carry you over till quarter-day, and there will be the expenses connected with moving, and so forth. How much?—say three! You know we can always get more, if you run short."

" But supposing that you are unable to meet those bills?" ventured Arthur.

"Why, then, we must renew again," answered Mr. Black, cheerily, "and renew, and renew, and renew till one or other of us comes into his fortune. We cannot be kept out of it for ever," added Mr. Black, jocularly. There was no having this man; once afloat with him, no one need ever after expect to touch solid land—once launched in the same boat, and you had to obey Captain Black, who would have laughed while sending one of the crew to his death, and kept "up the steam" had his nearest friend been dying.

Spite of his good spirits, however, Arthur ventured to interrogate him concerning the marketable value of paid-up shares, as to which the promoter's opinion was almost identical with that of Mr. Stewart.

"But they are available as security," proceeded Mr. Black. "For instance, if you were pushed for money, you could get an advance upon them. They are much the same as Berrie Down, you understand, tangible property—something to show, if a creditor turns crusty, or discount rises too high. We shall, all of us, do very well yet; and I am glad you are coming to town. You will never care to go back to Hertfordshire afterwards, even when you are worth ten thousand a year. Here are the stamps; that is right. Now, Dudley, I must trouble you for a moment. Let us first see the amounts, however, of those we must renew;" and Mr. Black, pulling out his pocket-book, consulted various memoranda which it contained, all having reference to certain of the bills coming due as fast as the autumn peaches ripen.

"I may as well give you a cheque for three hundred," said Mr. Black; "no need to be sending it down after you;" and Peter Black forthwith drew a cheque for three hundred pounds in favour of Arthur Dudley, Esquire, or order, which document he crossed, "Hertford and South Kemms' Banking Company."

Mr. Stewart would have known that he did this in order to give himself time to get some of Arthur's acceptances discounted before the cheque came back to his bankers ; but Squire Dudley, being less acquainted with business manœuvres than the great director, thought it was all in the ordinary course of affairs.

It did not occur to him either as singular that many of the bills he accepted should bear no drawer's signature attached—an omission Mr. Stewart would at once have detected and challenged.

Truth was, Mr. Black and the two Crossenhams played into each other's hands, thus : the Crossenhams would get a bill discounted at their bankers, the produce of which Black would then pay into his own bank. Then he would get a bill discounted, with Crossenhams' name to it as drawer, and hand that amount over to Crossenhams. Thus, the bills went dancing about like shuttlecocks—they were paid away, they were discounted, they were given as security, and nobody but Mr. Black knew for what exact sum Arthur had made himself liable.

"Enough to puzzle Berrie Down," said Mr. Black to himself, thoughtfully, as, after Arthur's departure, he totted up the amounts attached to the memoranda of which mention has previously been made; " enough to puzzle Berrie Down, if the ' Protector' come to grief; but it shall not do that, not, at any rate, until I have had my penn'orths out of it."

Having arrived at which prudent and honest conclusion, Mr. Black closed his pocket-book, circling it for extra security with an india-rubber band. That pocket-book, which never left Mr. Black's person except when he was asleep (and then he locked it up in a small safe in his dressing-room), contained all the present secrets of the promoter's life.

Had Mr. Stewart only obtained a sight of the pages that band kept so tightly together, he might reasonably have considered the ultimate success of the "Protector Bread and Flour Company, Limited," problematical.

CHAPTER X.

HOW HEATHER TOOK IT.

THE secretaryship was duly accepted, although not by letter; Arthur Dudley thought it best to call upon Mr. Stewart, and express in person his willingness to fill up the post offered.

Probably a secret pride influenced this determination. After a fashion, he was going to be the man's servant; but that was no reason why he should not return Mr. Stewart's call, and place himself on a footing of social equality with him.

For this reason, also, he did not walk from Dowgate Hill to King's Arm Yard, and take his chance of seeing Mr. Stewart at his office, as anybody else, standing less upon his dignity, might have done; but, at considerable inconvenience, repaired next afternoon to the great director's house, where, of course, he did not find him.

This, however, was a matter of secondary importance. The Squire had done the proper thing in the proper manner, and, having left his card, went back to Mr. Black's abode satisfied.

The same evening a messenger arrived in Stanley Crescent with a note from Mr. Stewart, expressive of regret at having missed seeing Mr. Dudley, and begging him to breakfast with the writer the following morning at ten o'clock.

"A business fellow," observed Mr. Black, approvingly, "and worth such a lot of money; I wonder who will have it when he dies. Croft, likely as not. Is there not some scripture about people who have much, getting more?"

Very heartily Arthur Dudley secretly anathematised this Croft, who seemed to be now, as he thought, for ever under his nose.

Already he was beginning to have personal experience of the truth Mr. Raidsford had mentioned to Lord Kemms—namely, that people always meet again; that, let the circle in which they revolve be large or small, still they ultimately come back to the point whence they started, and are brought once more into contact with the men and the women they knew at that period in their career.

If he please, a man may, like Arthur Dud.cy, curse the old ties, and strive to break away from them; but, like Arthur Dudley also, he will find after the years that there is no severance possible.

Friends and acquaintances; those whom we once knew well; those whom we have merely met, crop up continually in our path. We come across them in unlikely places; we encounter them in strange houses; we are thrown against them under the most singular circumstances. We leave them, as we think, behind, and behold, we discover, when the years roll by, that they have been travelling also; that, during all the time which seemed to be increasing the distance between us, we have really been traversing gradually converging lines, which bring us, after the springs, and the summers, and the autumns, and the winters, face to face at last.

Here, after years, for instance, was Squire Dudley brought into contact once again with the people he had known and dwelt among in his earlier manhood; here, also, he was going to breakfast with the bachelor of Scotch proclivities, who had so long ago influenced the name bestowed upon Heather at her baptism. Once more there was a likelihood of Mrs. Dudley reviving the associations of her childhood, and meeting with some of the members of her own kith and kin.

The Bells of Layford — amongst whom figured prominently a Sir Wingrave Bell — had long been friends of Mr. Allan Stewart.

Scottish people all, come southward, they hung together after the goodly manner of their country; and, very probably, had it not been for the unhappy quarrel which ended in utter alienation between the Rector of Layford, and his cousin and patron's eldest friend and ally, Mr. Stewart would have done well for his god-child when she was left an orphan, and not relinquished her without a struggle into the hands of Mrs. Travers, who had proved herself, perhaps, a little unduly anxious to be rid of such a trust.

As it was, when Mr. Bell died, Mr. Stewart chanced to be abroad. On his return he casually inquired what had become of the daughter, and being informed that her aunt had taken the orphan to her own home, let the matter drop out of his recollection. Of Heather's connection with Arthur

Dudley he was completely ignorant, and Arthur was not the man to acquaint him with it.

But yet, while the Squire sat opposite to his host at breakfast, he was wondering whether in due course of time, if the fact did by any chance come to Mr. Stewart's knowledge, it might not prove beneficial to' himself; induce the director to withdraw his opposition concerning the purchase of that " desirable house in Lincoln's Inn Fields, with yard at the back, over which a large room could be built (see advertisement), and the right of walking in the gardens of the Square."

Why this last clause always presented itself to Arthur Dudley's mind, it would be somewhat difficult to say, since a board of directors is not usually alive to the advantages of a "key to the Square;" but still, that it did present itself is unquestionable, and he thought about it while Mr. Stewart said he was glad to hear his visitor had decided not to press the matter on the Company, but to accept the secretaryship, and take up his residence in Lincoln's Inn.

" A very good situation for a dwelling," finished Mr. Stewart, who would as soon have thought of living in Lincoln's Inn as he would have thought

of flying; "and a good house too. You are married,
I presume?"

Arthur admitted the correctness of Mr. Stewart's
supposition.

"That is right; every man ought to marry," said
the bachelor. "Have you any children?"

"Two—a boy and girl," said the Squire; "one
of them is in very bad health. I do not know what
her mother will think about bringing her to town."

"You have not mentioned your intentions, then,
to Mrs. Dudley?" said Mr. Stewart, apparently
surprised.

"I thought it would be time enough to tell her
when the matter was settled," answered Arthur.

"Evidently, then, you will not consider it necessary to take your wife into your confidence concerning all the affairs of our Company?" suggested the
director.

"I do not think women ever understand anything
of business matters," Arthur replied; then, noticing
Mr. Stewart smile, he added, "and I am positive
my wife would not wish me to tell her any of the
affairs of my principals."

"I have heard of Mrs. Dudley as a lady of an
excellent discretion," said Mr. Stewart.

"You do not expect me to praise my own wife," answered Arthur, deprecating this praise; and the evasion was really rather a clever one for him. If he had praised her at all, however, it would simply have been as his wife, and because she belonged to him, not in her mere capacity as a woman.

Mr. Stewart felt curious about this Mrs. Dudley, whose husband so decidedly refused to speak of her. Miss Baldwin had been by no means so reticent. She had described Heather to her cousin, and told him all about the brothers and sisters who used to run wild before the young wife's arrival at Berrie Down. Lally also was not left out of the narrative. "The sweetest little creature in the world," the Honourable Augusta declared; "just the child you would love, Mr. Stewart."

"I never saw the child I loved yet," said the old bachelor, somewhat incredulously, "and I do not think I ever shall."

Notwithstanding this speech, however, Mr. Stewart had been secretly touched by Miss Baldwin's description of mother and child, which description caused him to form a mental picture of Mrs. Dudley that did not exactly frame in the setting Arthur now provided for her.

"Is this fellow such a weak fool as to be envious of his wife," thought the director; "or is there really some flaw in his pearl of which the little world of South Kemms is not cognisant?" Mr. Stewart could not understand his companion's domestic relations, so he thought he would try him on another tack—his children.

"I heard something, when I was at Kemms Park, about your little girl having met with an accident," he began.

"Yes, she fell into that mill-pond at the bottom of my farm, and was nearly drowned," Arthur replied, shortly.

"She has been very ill since that, though, has she not?" asked Mr. Stewart, who was beginning to think his visitor carried his ideas of politeness a little too far.

"Very ill; but she is now out of danger."

"Do you think of bringing her up to town?"

"That will be a question for her mother to decide."

"Was there ever such a prig before!" thought the director; but he said out loud, "Then you take nothing to do with such minor matters?"

"Nothing," answered Arthur, decidedly; "my wife has had a vast amount of anxiety concerning the child, and I should not like to interfere; though, I should think," added the Squire, "that if once we could get her up to London and under better medica. treatment, she would soon be well again."

"Why do you not take a doctor down to see her?" asked Mr. Stewart.

"The expense," murmured his guest.

"True, I had forgotten," said the director apologetically; but while he meditatively finished his tea, he remembered the money Arthur had advanced to Mr. Black, and spent uselessly on the purchase of the house he now proposed occupying.

"I presume that, whether or not Mrs. Dudley come to town at once, you can enter on the duties of your new post immediately?" Mr. Stewart said, at length.

"Certainly; if my wife be afraid of leaving home, one of my sisters must come up and keep house for me."

"You have sisters, then?"

This was enough; that question speedily loosened Arthur's tongue; on that portion of his family history he was never—the chance of speaking being given to him—dumb.

" Yes, he had sisters, but they were not his own, they were sisters by a second marriage. His father had made a most imprudent choice of a wife without money or connection, who brought five children into the world that I," said Arthur, " have had to clothe, educate, and support. That is what has kept me a poor man. For thirteen years I have had that burden to carry. You cannot wonder at my being as I am. One of the boys has now got a situation, but he is only earning thirty pounds a year, and that will not do much towards keeping him. You perceive how necessary it is for me to add to my income. With my own children growing up, it is impossible for me to avoid feeling uneasy."

" Your sisters will marry?" suggested Mr. Stewart.

" I do not know who is to marry them," said Arthur, ruefully.

" People do not know generally, until the right man comes," said the bachelor, laughing.

Arthur struck him as being eminently absurd. It was long since he had come in contact with a man he more thoroughly despised; but, all unconscious of the impresssion he was producing, Arthur went on talking of his grievances, of how badly fortune had treated him, and Mr. Stewart encouraged such talk. He wanted to know of what stuff his companion was made; and so Arthur proceeded, without the faintest idea crossing his mind that he was revealing himself all the while in a most unfavourable light; that there was not a speck, or flaw, or weak point, in his most weak character, which his host was not examining critically and cynically.

Away from Heather, away from that most beautifying influence, which made even his faults seem errors, to be lightly viewed and tenderly treated for the sake of the love she bore him; away from the wife, who was unto him as a crown giving some faint semblance of man's royalty to that poor weak brow, Arthur stood confessed for what he was—a feeble, impulsive, wearisome, selfish egotist, who had a quarrel with the world, because, while it contained rich and poor, and he did not stand amongst the former; who laid the burden of his ill-success on every back save his own; who would not look on the bright side of his actual existence, but had suffered himself to be led away after a will-o'-the-wisp by Mr. Black, and who lacked, as Mr. Stewart delicately implied to him, sense and energy sufficient to make a good thing of his life, and a good income out of Berrie Down.

" You have no rent to pay," said the director; " it seems to me you might have got a fortune out of that lovely place of yours, had you only gone to work thoroughly."

" How ?" asked Arthur, helplessly.

" How ? why, how do other people make money out of land—make money and pay heavy rents into the bargain?   Do not think me impertinent, if I say I would rather have trusted to the sense and gratitude of Berrie Down Hollow than of Mr. Black."

Arthur could not help thinking Mr. Stewart not merely impertinent but foolish, although he replied,

" I do not think there is much money to be made by farming."

" Don't you !" said Mr. Stewart. " I fancy I have made more money by farming than by anything else; but, however, no doubt you know your own business best—every man does."

Arthur imagined he did, at any rate ; nevertheless,

he left Mr. Stewart with a certain depression of spirit, which was, however, in due time chased away by Mr. Black.

"Come up again!" said that gentleman. "No, you need not; deuce a bit of necessity for anything of the kind. Leave all to me. I'll see the house is ready for you; Mrs. Black will send in a charwoman, and all that sort of thing. I shouldn't move even a table from Berrie Down; nothing but plate and linen. No use breaking up a home. You'll want to run down there occasionally from Saturday till Monday. We'll all run down. Should not go to the expense; you will furnish as cheaply as you could move your sticks. Leave all to me. I'll not put you to unnecessary expense; but you know you must have decent furniture about you. Servants! Oh, better let Mrs. Dudley see to them—whatever messenger we have can be made useful as footman also, remember. You'll charge him to the Company, as well as coals, gas, taxes, and so forth. By Jove! Dudley, it will be a first-rate thing for you. Living free, as one may say, and drawing a thousand a year. I'll get the painters and paper-hangers in at once, and report progress. The place shall be ready for you in a fortnight. There, there, no thanks; tut, tut, man, don't make a fuss over such a trifle. Good-bye! Remember me to Mrs. Dudley. Good-bye!" and, amid much waving of hands and excited adieux, the train steamed out of the station, and Arthur was off for Palinsbridge, while Mr. Black returned to the City.

All the way down Arthur thought how he should best break the news to Heather. It seemed to him now, that if he had only made a confidante of her all along, his way would have proved easier. He should now have to tell her the whole from the beginning, or at least as much of the whole as he ever meant to tell her. How he had listened to the voice of the charmer; how the charmer had given him shares in the Protector Bread Company, Limited; how he had been offered the secretary-ship of that thriving company; how he thought a thousand a year much too good a chance to be re-fused; how he had promised Mr. Stewart to enter on his duties at once; how there was a house in Lincoln's Inn Fields, rented by the Company, which they were to inhabit.

He would have to tell her all this, but he need tell her no more; he need not add how foolish and trustful he had been; he need make no mention of bills or money; there was no necessity for him to say anything about the house in Lincoln's Inn, which he had purchased.

As for Berric Down, to which some one must see, could not Mrs. Piggott take charge of it? Mrs. Piggott and Ned. Suppose Ned and Mrs. Piggott made a match of it.

Mrs. Piggott had, indeed, if all accounts were to be believed, led her deceased husband such a "devil of a life," that he was glad, after three years' patient endurance of her temper, to skulk under ground to get rid of it; but then those days lay very far back in the woman's life; she had been forced to struggle with the world; she had buried two children; she had "supped sorrow with the spoon of grief," and there are some natures to whom sorrow taken in any form proves a very wholesome medicine.

It had done so in Mrs. Piggott's case; the years had softened her, tamed her spirit, subdued her temper. She would have made a very good wife to any one wanting an elderly managing woman to cook his dinner and keep his house tidy; a very good wife indeed for Ned, who had worshipped his lost and lamented Polly—a "fine woman," large, well-developed, and handsome, whose only fault was mildly represented by Ned to have been, that her delicate health obliged her to take more gin than was always good for her.

Like Mr. Piggott, Polly had long been slumbering where gin is not procurable; and thus Squire Dudley's idea concerning a match being got up between the pair was perfectly feasible, and likely, so he thought, to meet the views of all parties interested in the matter.

Mrs. Piggott was faithful and trustworthy. So also was Mr. Edward Byrne, a gentleman of Irish extraction on his father's side—a soft, willing, hard-working fellow, full of odd sayings, and possessed of unfailing spirits, which kept him continually at high pressure, and ready at all times for anything, "from pitch-and-toss to manslaughter."

Byrne could saddle a horse, and ride it afterwards; harness one or a pair, and drive it or them likewise; he could churn and he would pump; he darned his own stockings, and he cobbled his own shoes. He was always up betimes in the morning, and could be depended on to see to the feeding of the sheep and the foddering of the cattle. To Ned was intrusted the key of the oat-bin, and he always presided over the brewing of the ale. It was he who had the mowers at work by four o'clock in the summer's mornings, whilst the grass was still wet and heavy with dew; he who stacked the oats and went to market for Squire Dudley. And yet, Ned was not proud. Mrs. Piggott objected to young men and boys about the house, so he did not disdain cleaning the knives and polishing the boots, singing to himself all the while like a perfect nightingale, or else talking to Mrs. Piggott or the servants, and recounting to them tales of a far remote period in his life when he was "devil" in a printing-office, and had to "cut about" with proof.

Then, Ned had acquired literary tastes and a knowledge of minstrelsy, which made him a perfect treasure at harvest-homes, sheep-shearings, and such-like. Amongst his class he was considered an orator, and it is greatly to be questioned whether Mario was ever more warmly applauded than Mr. Byrne, when at the festive board he "favoured the company" with "Auld Lang Syne."

A true diplomatist, he always selected songs which would bear a chorus, well knowing that the true secret of personal popularity is to induce every one to believe that some portion of that popularity is reflected on him or her.

A man is, as a rule, much more heartily clapped when the audience feel they are clapping themselves at the same time—clapping their own talents, sentiments, virtues; and Ned's admirers accordingly stamped their feet, and hammered on the table with their spoons and knives in precise proportion as the chorus to Mr. Byrne's melody had been long, loud, and discordant.

· After leaving the printing-office, which he quitted, because, as he stated, the hours kept by authors were bad for his constitution, he obtained a situation with a lawyer residing in the Temple, whose hours proved to be still worse than those affected by the authors with whom Ned had previously associated.

"You might get some sleep in the one case, drop off in the hall, or have forty winks sitting on the stairs, but with Mr. Froom there was rest neither day nor night," he said; so, finding that town habits were not to his mind, that he had to work harder in London than " anybody ever was asked to work in the country," Ned, then a stunted, pale-faced, sickly lad, resolved to cut the undesirable acquaintance of members both of the literary and legal professions, and return home to those peaceful shades where, in former days, he had digested fat bacon, cheese in quantity, and—

> " Home-made bread
> As heavy as lead;"

to say nothing of various other delicacies: such as batter and Yorkshire puddings, treacle roll-up, bubble-and-squeak, toad-in-the-hole, harslet-pie, and liver-and-crow—fearful combinations, which are all as appetising to the agricultural classes as the daintiest dishes of a French *chef* to the upper ten thousand.

Upon this fare, Ned, in the pure country air, throve and grew apace, and when, in due time, he took service with Major Dudley, of Berrie Down, he was a fine, strapping fellow, willing and able to do almost anything in the way of farm labour, and not above putting his hand to whatever his hand found to do. He had been " odd and useful man " at

Berrie Down so long back as the memory of Arthur Dudley extended. His hair had grown grey from the passage of years spent at the Hollow, and not, as he facetiously informed young women, from its having stayed out too long in the wet one night and got mouldy.

He was faithful and unambitious; but, nevertheless, he had money to the good in South Kemms Bank,—a fact which it is fortunate Mr. Black never suspected, or he might, in the course of his wanderings over the farm, and long discourses with Ned, have induced him to go in for shares, and inoculated man as well as master with a mania for speculation.

Mrs. Piggott, likewise, had saved money. Why should the pair not marry, and unite their common earnings against the day when more work for either would be impossible? Ned would make a good husband to any woman; Mrs. Piggott would see to his meals and his comforts, and, perhaps, not be too hard upon him if he did take a pint too much ale at any of the rustic gatherings.

Why should they not marry? why, at all events, should they not be put in charge? That is, if

Heather objected, as Arthur feared she would, to leaving the girls and Cuthbert at the Hollow; while he, and she, and Lally, and Leonard, went up to town.

"Fact is," was the solemn truth with which Squire Dudley came home after his mental excursion, "I never ought to have married. See how it ties a man at the most important crisis of his life!"

Having arrived at which pleasant conclusion, Arthur reached Palinsbridge, where Ned and a horse awaited him.

As he rode homeward he pondered over and over how he should best "break the news" to Heather. Any one following his train of reflection might have thought Mrs. Dudley was a perfect virago, so much did her husband dread her reception of the intelligence that he had accepted the secretaryship, and meant, for the future, to reside in London.

Almost he wished he had asked Mr. Black to come down and make the communication for him. He knew Heather would not scold, or nag, or strive to render him miserable about the matter, but he knew also she would feel hurt at his reserve, his secrecy, his want of trustfulness.

Long ago she had asked him not to let them drift away one from the other—what had she meant by that? Was it possible Heather should ever become reserved towards him? that her love should ever grow less? her devotion ever dwindle and die away altogether? Was what his aunt had told him at Copt Hall true?—" You will not be able to retain Heather's affection for ever, Arthur, if you give her none in return. You have got a wife such as no man ever found before; take care lest you sustain a loss such as no man ever can repair."

What did it mean? Arthur Dudley pulled up his horse to a walk, and asked himself this question as he entered Berrie Down Lane.

He had heard men say they never valued a mother's love till it could be given to them never more. Was this what Miss Hope desired to imply? Did she think Heather delicate? Did she imagine there was any fear of her fading away and leaving him? What would his life be without Heather? Who would ever again bear with him, think for him, love him, like the woman whom he now feared to face,—whom he now rode slowly on to meet, slowly though he knew she was waiting and watching for his arrival?

What a game of cross-purposes love is altogether! What a stake some people throw down on the board, what despairing losers many walk forth again into the world!

Make your game, gentlemen, make your game, it is all a matter of business! The world must not stand still, even though hearts be broken.

Make your game! The game is made, and here is the result: a great intellect mated to a fool, a fond woman mismatched with a weak, or brutal, or unloving husband!

What, complaining? You played for happiness and you have lost. There are other gamblers coming forward—pray stand aside.

Or it is a lottery, and the people come up to draw. Only a doll, only an idiot, a shrew, a tyrant, a faithless husband, a coquettish wife, a plausible pretender: a woman all paint and padding, all affectation and extravagance, — a man polished enough in his manners, yet coarse and repulsive in the ordinary course of every-day domestic life!

And you grumble? Pray, Sir, and Madam, did you not pay your money and take your chance?

Have you not drawn *something* out of the matrimonial lottery? It does not suit you? Oh! we can have no exchanges here! there are your goods, take them. "Here's a lottery in which no man draws a blank!" and so forth till the end of time; so forth, while the men and the women go home with their purchases, and shrine them or curse them, according as the goods suit or their tempers incline.

What a game of cross-purposes! what a lottery of incongruous chances! What a singular thing that Arthur and Heather should ever have married! What a still more marvellous affair, that only after the years, the possibility should occur to him of her affection weakening, of her love decaying!

What an awful mistake it is men and women alike make, when they imagine that because love has been, love will be, always!

As though there were any human attachment which constant dropping could not wear away; as though the devotion existed which neglect and distrust, unkindness and coldness, would not ultimately alienate!

Can the tendrils go on for ever feeling after a support which is removed from them? Will there not come a day when they will either wither away, or otherwise turn elsewhere for something around which to twine? Was that what Miss Hope meant? or did she only intend to imply that one day, when he wanted the love, and the help, and the companionship he now spurned, he should stretch forth his hands in vain to meet only vacancy?

Strange things often ride beside a man, keep his company in the night watches, walk with him along the familiar paths; strange things the ghosts of "what has been," the shadows of "what is to be;" and it was most probably a mixture of both these phantoms that caused Squire Dudley to spur his horse, shying in the moonlight—on—and to push forward more rapidly under the elms and the beeches, beside the hedge-rows, bare of flower and leaf, across the gleaming brook—home.

Where Heather was waiting for him with the old glad look of welcome in her face, with the soft pleading tone in her voice, with the half timid touch laid on his shoulder, "so pleased to see him home again," she said; "so thankful to be able to tell him Lally was better—much better, and she herself quite rested. Had he been well, and had he settled his business satisfactorily?" He was seated before the fire by this time with his top-coat off, and his feet stretched out towards the warmth.

He was at home, and the little bustle of arrival over. The inevitable moment had come at last— the moment when, if he ever were to tell his wife of the impending change, the communication must be made.

And yet, looking round, it did seem hard to break up that pleasant home, to leave the familiar places, and strive to set up the household gods of Berrie Down on a strange shrine—in strange niches.

The shadows which had pursued him up the Lane must have entered at the open door and sat down beside the Squire, for there was something, not merely of dread, but also of regret, in his heart, when turning, he said to Heather,—

" I have news for you."

" Good news," she said ; " anything about Bessie?"

" No, nothing to do with any one but ourselves. As for whether my news be good or bad, I cannot tell, for that will depend somewhat on how you take it. What should you say if I told you I had added a thousand a year to our income?"

"I should say it was almost too good to be true," she answered.

"But it is true," he said, "only there is one draw- back—we must leave Berrie Down."

"Leave Berrie Down!" she repeated.

"I do not mean leave it entirely," he explained : "but still, for a considerable part of each year, it will be necessary for us to reside in town. We shall have a large house there, rent free, and——"

"Tell me what it all means, Arthur," she said, interrupting his confused sentence. "Begin at the beginning, and explain it to me. Where is this thousand a year coming from ? Why is it necessary we should live in town ?"

She knelt down beside him as she spoke : knelt down, and leaning her elbows on the arm of the chair he occupied, looked up in his face, with those lovely, pleading, sad eyes, that had still the brooding sorrow in them.

For the first time, that expression struck Arthur painfully; that expression of all not being happy in her life, which it is so bitter a thing to behold in the face of any one near and dear to us ; that expres- sion of terrible though almost unconscious loneliness, which is so pitif l, so pathetic, we can scarcely look upon it without tears.

Once more let me paint her for you as she kneels there in the fire-light,—let me paint her in the very prime of her womanhood, with the rich warm tints of her hair contrasting against her clear white skin, with her small ears peeping out from below the heavy braids which were wreathed round and round her head, with her face uplifted towards Arthur, her lips parted, her hands clasped, and that pleading look in her eyes—that look which had in it something of a dumb appeal — of an entreaty, which, although the heart could conceive, the tongue refused to utter.

Before he could answer her, Arthur had to turn his head away, and fix his eyes on the dancing fire-light. Passing through the world's long picture gallery, it is oftentimes not the great paintings, not the court ceremonials, not the huge sea pieces, not the representations of battle-fields, not the important portraits and the historical incidents which are photographed on our memories, which are stamped on our mental retina so indelibly, that through the years they are never forgotten. It is not the large finished pictures which we went out to see, which we took, perhaps, much notice of at the time, that stay with us and remain in our memories longest; rather it is the figure of some beggar child, the little glimpse of woodland scenery, the barren bleakness of some desolate moor, the hopeless languor of a dying man's hand,—these are the trifles which, God knows why, we carry away with us. The scenes of great account at which we have been present, on which we have gazed, in which, perchance, we have been actors, pale and fade away from the canvas of our brains; but so long as memory remains, there are slight gestures and passing expressions which recur to us again and again, and which will recur, till life leave us and the mould be heaped up over the spot where we lie.

The tone of a voice, the look in a face, the pressure of a hand, a chance word spoken in love or in anger, a stray sentence in a book—these things stay with us when, to our thinking, weightier matters are forgotten, when the passions and the sorrows, the struggles and the successes of the years departed have come to be in our recollections but as a flower which has bloomed—a leaf which has faded.

Many a time in the after-days, when all the important events and exciting interviews of that period of his life had become blurred and indistinct, there would rise up before Arthur Dudley's mental sight a vision of a woman kneeling beside him in the fire-light, of a soft, tender voice entreating him to tell her all—of white hands clasped tightly, in mute supplication—of eyes uplifted, pleading for a fuller confidence, for more perfect faith and love.

Did he give her any one of the things she thus silently asked for? Ah! it is hard for a man who has started on a wrong road to retrace his steps; it is well-nigh impossible for any one who has been led on, and on, from less to more, from little to much, to go back to the beginning, and explain circumstantially how he has gradually become entangled, deeper and deeper; how, meaning to put forth for only a short sail, he has drifted away to lands he never intended visiting—to shores where he encountered strange people and formed undesirable acquaintances, destined to change the whole course of his life, to make a difference in his career here, and, it may be—who can tell?—in his state hereafter.

So he was not frank, and the chance of a full and free understanding between the husband and wife ebbed back among the waves, to be restored by them no more.

He told her precisely what he had determined to tell: he said he had been offered the secretary-ship; that he considered it too good a proposal to refuse, and so he closed with it at once. He was eloquent concerning the relief such a salary must bring; he described all the advantages a residence in town would ensure; was fluent about the house in Lincoln's Inn Fields—the wide staircase, the lofty rooms, the airy situation, the pleasant gardens of the Square; and then he wound up by saying, that the only drawback to his perfect happiness and con-tentment in the matter, was his fear lest Heather should object to living in town—lest, being so much attached to Berrie Down, she should dislike leaving it.

As he said this he took courage and turned and looked at her, and, behold! the sad, lonely expres-sion was gone, and another, more difficult, perhaps, to analyze, had come in its place.

"Arthur," she answered, and the low, sweet

voice—in which, as I wrote once before, there was a great virtue of leisure—was broken neither by sorrow nor passion, as she spoke, "I love Berrie Down much, but I love you better; I had not seen this place when I married you. You need not be afraid of it parting us now."

And that was all! The dreaded confession was made, and this was how she took it. Could anything have been quieter, calmer, more satisfactory? Yes; if she had been vexed and angry, Arthur could have understood her better. If she had cross-questioned him, and uttered reproaches about his not having previously made a confidante of her, he would have escaped that sense of something being amiss which fell like ice upon his heart.

He could not know what a world of feeling was contained in the short sentence she had uttered. How should he know? this man who never took his wife in his arms, when she said she loved him better than Berrie Down; nor told how she was more to him than houses and lands—than gold and silver; who allowed her to rise from the ground and stand looking steadfastly into the fire, and only marvelled what she could be thinking of—where on earth her mind was wandering.

Already that scene was for both of them a thing of the past; already the lichens and the mosses of memory were growing around, and taking the fresh bareness off it, destroying the harshness of the cold, grey outline.

But half an hour before, and the news had still to be imparted; and now the tidings were told and received, and all difficulty was over; all doubt of her concurrence removed.

Down the gallery of Time already the footsteps of the past were echoing, carrying away that scene from memory, in order to fling it into the lumber-room containing life's unused opportunities.

It had been with him but a moment before to be employed as a shield and a buckler, as a safeguard from trouble, as a sword against the enemy; and, behold, the man was so blind, so feeble, so incompetent, as to let it slip from his fingers, and glide away to be seized and borne off, and recalled no more, save in sorrowful memories with unavailing regrets.

For when return to the land is impossible, even

the most reckless will perceive the extent of the danger he has courted, and stretch forth his hands despairingly towards that fair shore which is receding from his gaze for ever.

CHAPTER XI.

LEAVING BERRIE DOWN.

THE programme of domestic arrangements which Arthur Dudley had so ingeniously sketched out, as he travelled from London to Palinsbridge, was, like many other programmes, destined to undergo much revision before being presented to the public.

In the first place, Mrs. Piggott's prudence, or possibly, even her morality, objected to being left alone with Ned at Berrie Down in charge of that establishment. A house without a mistress had always been Mrs. Piggott's special abhorrence,—a house where things, as she said, " ran wild."

Further, Mrs. Dudley most earnestly desired that if her lot were to be cast in town, it should not be cast there in company with strange servants; and, after much anxious discussion, it was accordingly agreed that Susan should take Mrs. Piggott's position, and a new housemaid be engaged to fill Jane's place, while Prissy and Jane and Mrs. Piggott accompanied the family to London. As an almost necessary consequence of this arrangement, it was decided that Agnes and Laura should remain at the Hollow; Agnes willingly undertaking to "see to things" as much as possible, and write Heather an account of the farm proceedings every week.

Ned, of course, was to take charge of out-door matters, as hitherto; and Lucy and Cuthbert were to proceed to town.

It seemed to Mr. Black, when he heard these various decisions, that the whole family must suddenly have taken leave of their senses.

"Why the deuce you could not have put in a care-taker, and sold the cows, and got rid of all the poultry, and let that Ned fellow see to the ploughing and sowing, passes my comprehension. The girls will never get married down there; why, I don't suppose they see a man from one year's end to another!"

"There is one of them coming up, remember," said Arthur Dudley, in a tone of apology, as though

some excuse were necessary for not putting his
sisters in the way of matrimonial chances; "and
Heather and they settled it, somehow, amongst
them. It appeared to me rather a good arrangement."

"Well, it may be, if you wish to have them on
your hands for ever," answered Mr. Black; at
which remark Arthur bit his lip.

He did not like being interfered with, or advised
overmuch. If he wished his sisters to stay at Berrie
Down, what business was it of Mr. Black's whether
they remained there or not? He had maintained
them when no other member of the family could or
would have done so, and he did not see that any
person had a right to make comments on what he
did or left undone.

"You need not look crusty, Squire," proceeded
Mr. Black; "what I said is merely my opinion, and
you may take it for what it is worth; only I consider it to be a confoundedly bad plan to have two
establishments, and so I tell you. I would shut up
Berrie Down, and move the whole party, bag and
baggage, to town. That is what I should do; but,
of course, you can do as you like."

" Yes; and that is what I intend to do: much obliged, at the same time, for your kind permission."

" Hoity-toity !" said Mr. Black, taking off his hat, and bowing low as he spoke ;—it was in one of the empty rooms of Arthur's house in Lincoln's Inn Fields that this conversation occurred,—"hoity-toity ! your most obedient, sir, and humbly beg pardon for the liberty."

In a pet, Arthur turned away, and walking to one of the windows, looked out over the Square, while Mr. Black regarded him with a smile, in which there lurked not merely amusement, but also triumph and contempt.

" You're a nice chicken, you are," thus ran the promoter's secret thought; " and you have a sweet temper, Mister Squire Dudley ; and you think you are able to manage your affairs, though anybody, willing to take the trouble, might put a ring through your nose, and lead you from here to Jericho. And so you intend to do as you like ! It will be as *I* like before we have done with one another, I fancy ; a conceited, upsetting ass !"

But Mr. Black was much too wise a man to allow even a word of all this to pass his lips. He had his game still to play; and he would not mar the chances of success by any irritated or indiscreet remark.

"Come, Dudley," he said, "we are not going to quarrel over trifles, are we? I meant no offence, and am sorry if you have taken any. I have knocked about the world too much to be as mealy-mouthed as most of your acquaintances, but I should be as sorry to vex you, perhaps, as any of them. I am glad you like the papers I have chosen; you will find everything in apple-pie order when you bring up Mrs. Dudley and the children. So your wife is going to try moving Miss Lally? I am glad of it; I believe she will get well in half the time in town."

That was what Heather trusted also; she hoped that some of the great doctors in London would be able to do more for her little girl in a month than the general practitioner at Fifield had effected in five. Every one told her she was doing the wisest thing possible in taking Lally to town! every one was so kind and good!

Mrs. Poole Seymour sent her carriage to convey mother and child to the station, and Mr. Plimpton was at Palinsbridge, ready to conduct Lally across the bridge, and deposit her safely in the compartment he had secured for the travellers.

Miss Baldwin promised to call upon the girls "very often," and said she should not "forget to find her way to Lincoln's Inn when in town ;" while Mrs. Raidsford came lumbering over in the great family chariot, and, not to be outdone in neighbourly thoughtfulness and delicate consideration, brought Heather a basket of the worst grapes growing in the Moorlands conservatory, and offered to lend her " one of the footmen," if he could be of any service in seeing to her luggage.

It was fortunate for Heather she had, towards the last, so many people to see, so many things to occupy and distract her mind, or else that parting from Berrie Down, when the spring flowers were budding, when the fresh leaves were clothing all the trees, when the birds were singing on every branch and bough, must almost have broken her heart.

She loved the spring-time—that time which always seems more full of hope, and joy, and life, and promise than any other period in the year. It had been her delight, ever since she came to Berrie

Down, to watch the buds gradually forming, to peep with the children at the nests, where eggs, speckled, and blue, and white, and green, were covered by birds that rarely took fright at sight of the familiar faces; to her, the lambing season was the pleasantest of the four—the long, long summer stretched away beyond the spring, and the rich, glowing autumn beyond that, and all these good things were to be had and enjoyed before the winter, with its leafless trees, with its snows and frosts, with its rain and storms, came again to Berrie Down.

To any person passionately fond of the country, of its sights, and sounds, and pleasures, the coming of spring is as the beginning of a feast, as the sunrise on the morning of a bright glad holiday. To Heather, this had always been the happiest, most delicious time at Berrie Down—these months when the lambs commenced to dot the fields, when the daisies perked up their faces among the green grass, when the hyacinths began to bud in the dells, when the "sunny celandine" opened on the hedge-bank, when the children gathered branches of the crab-apple, when the first broods of chickens chipped their shells and went chirruping and scratching about the warmest corners of the farm-yard—when the sun really had some power, when the fruit-trees were in blossom and the lilacs showed for flower, when the tiger-lily reared its head in the garden, when every hedge-row was clad in its fresh robe of green, and there was that nameless scent of spring pervading that air—that scent with which the summer odours vainly strive to compete.

With a new sense of happiness upon her, with a sensuous delight in the soft balmy air, in the fragrance which pervaded the atmosphere, in the sunny smile which shone on the face of Nature, in the sudden stir which there seemed on every bough, in every blade of grass—Heather, I say, when all the things I have mentioned came to pass, would stand at the open window of the drawing-room, looking down over the Hollow, and away to the woods surrounding Kemms' Park, repeating to herself the while—

"The winter is past—the rain is over and gone—the flowers appear on the earth—the time for the singing-birds is come—and the voice of the turtle is heard in the land."

And now this time was come, and she had to leave it behind.

Just when the hawthorn-buds were forming—when the chestnut-trees were clothing themselves in great masses of foliage, to be relieved presently and lighted up with cone after cone of pure white flowers—when the laburnums were about loosening their golden curls, and the lilacs bethought themselves of filling the air with a delicious fragrance—when the westeria was hanging out its purple clusters, and the pyracanthas at the gate were a perfect sheet of bloom—when the white anemone and the starry stitchworth dotted the woods—when everything was looking its loveliest, and brightest, and purest, Heather was compelled to leave the place her heart had grown to during the years of her married life.

For some time previously, Arthur had been resident in town; but Mrs. Dudley, having many preparations to make, many arrangements to complete, remained at Berrie Down, not merely until the spring blossoms were come, but also until Lally was sufficiently recovered to travel.

The child still kept weakly and delicate; her once tireless limbs now refused to carry her for any long period. If she started to run along one of the garden walks, she soon returned to her mother with,

"Carry me, pease—legs ache." The colour did not return to her cheeks, nor strength to her body, neither did she get plump and soft again, as Heather hoped would have been the case.

The poor wasted arms, and little white face, and thin slight figure, had a pleading pitifulness about them, which the child's eager desire for exercise, her unquenched vivacity, made more pathetic still.

Whatever Lally saw any other creature doing, that she desired to essay also. She wanted to run after the lambs, and scamper like the dogs, and be out over the fields with Cuthbert, and trotting behind Agnes and Mrs. Piggott, to dairy, and poultry-yard, and paddock; but it was not to be! The spirit was there—strong, restless, excitable as ever; but the body was changed. No more gallops for Lally on any one's shoulder—no more charming excursions in Ned's wheelbarrow—no more clambering up ladders, and lofty thrones on the top of hay-stacks and corn-ricks—no more playing at hide-and-seek in the hollow—no more running after the ducks, and shrill laughter at seeing them take to the water in order to escape the pursuit of their tiny persecu-tor—no more searchings after hens that had stolen

away to lay—no more of these old happinesses for
Lally. Sickness had caught her one day, when his
advent was least looked for—caught and put her in
a cage, which would not permit her to move far in
any direction, against the bars of which the little restless heart fluttered and beat only to its own hurt—a
cage from which no human hand could release her,
though loving friends were all around, and kindly
eyes, often with tears in them, regarded the im-
patient child.

Tired—tired—always tired! Many and many a
time, when Heather, hearing this plaint, lifted her
child in her arms, she had to turn aside lest Lally
should see she was weeping; but one day Lally,
peeping round, beheld the tears on her mother's
face, and said—

" 'Oo crying, ma?—is it about Lally? Big, fat
lady told Lally she'll get some-sing when she goes
to London, that will make her better as well. When
are we going, ma—when?"

And because her own hopes were identical with
Lally's words, Mrs. Dudley did not grieve so much
concerning leaving Berrie Down as might otherwise
have been the case. As regarded the increase of

income, the prospect of greater pecuniary comfort, Heather felt no elation whatever.

If Arthur were satisfied, she could easily make herself satisfied also; but she had little faith that anything in which Mr. Black figured as prime mover would ultimately prove advantageous to her husband.

Besides, if a person have half a million a year, he can but be happy; and Heather knew perfectly well that the secret of being happy, even on two hundred a year, is to be satisfied therewith.

Arthur had never been contented, and she was quite aware that the increase to his income could not make him so. She understood her husband's peculiarities sufficiently by this time to know that his wants would only grow with what they fed on.

If Mr. Black's cry were always more capital, Arthur's had always been a larger revenue.

Looking back over her married life with eyes from which the glamour of early love was now completely cleared away, Heather saw that money matters might have been better with them for years past, had Arthur only been energetic, and strong, and determined, like other men—had he finished his draining instead of leaving it half completed—had he turned up his land and laid out money by degrees, as he could spare it, on that which never proves ungrateful for capital wisely expended, for care judiciously bestowed.

She could not be blind to the fact that, as a rule, they had bought stock dear and sold it cheap—that what Alick had often said, "Arthur is neither master nor man: neither master to give orders and see them carried out, nor man to obey orders if given by anybody else," was true.

There was no fairy mist hanging before her mental vision now. Like Mr. Stewart, she feared the person who could not make money at Berrie Down, plainly and economically as they had lived for years, would not be likely to make or to keep much money elsewhere. Certainly the thousand a year was something tangible—a peg on which to hang her faith, had any faith been left; but, like most women who have passed all the most important years of their lives in the country, Heather entertained a perfect horror of the expenses of living in town.

She did not believe one sentence of what Mr.

Black said about an income going as far there as in the country. She knew, no one better, how very small a money outlay had sufficed to maintain the family at Berrie Down comfortably and respectably.

Those only who have eaten of the fat of their own lands, and beheld the wheat growing which is afterwards to be ground into flour—who have scarcely missed from amongst the rough abundance of all farm produce, the poultry and milk, the butter, eggs, hams, vegetables, and meat necessary for the consumption even of a large family—can tell what a very difficult thing it is to cater for an establishment in town, where everything, to the country imagination, seems sold according to its weight in gold— where a housekeeper's hand is never out of her pocket from one week's end to another—where it is either bills or cash, but, in any case, ultimately money—where even a few sprigs of parsley, even a bunch of savoury herbs, cannot be procured without purchase, without going through the ceremony of buying that which, at the old home, grew wild, almost, along the sunniest borders—wild, to be had for the mere trouble of gathering.

Of that mongrel country life which exists in the

suburbs of great towns, and which has given rise to
various sayings concerning home-laid eggs at a
shilling a-piece, carrots at half-a-guinea the bunch,
butter half-a-crown a pound, and milk eighteen-
pence a quart, Heather had no experience. She
only knew that her father's glebe lands and Arthur's
farm had enabled their respective families to make
both ends meet, without pinching in the parlour, or
an over-strict and painful economy in the kitchen;
and she dreaded entering on what was to her an
utterly untried career—that of managing a town
establishment, and entering every item, from cream
to laundry work, in her formerly easily-kept house-
keeping book.

All these matters she had discussed, after a
woman's diffuse fashion, with Agnes and Mrs.
Piggott; and Agnes and Mrs. Piggott had both
agreed that much might still be forwarded from
Berrie Down; that it would only be Ned's time and
the pony's to run over to Palinsbridge with a weekly
hamper for town; "and besides, you will be often
down yourself, I hope, Heather," added Agnes; but
Heather shook her head.

"The expense," she said, "will be more than I

should like to incur frequently. I am afraid, although a thousand a year sounds a great deal, it will not go very far in London, more especially in the style Arthur talks of living."

" But his shares, you know, Heather?" suggested Agnes, hopefully.

" Yes, I had forgotten them," was the reply, evidently intended to be affirmative of the girl's cheerful views, but failing of its purpose, because Mrs. Dudley's tone implied that, now she did remember the shares, her spirits were not unduly raised.

She had heard too many revelations from Mrs. Black to be mightily exalted at the idea of being even indirectly connected with a company. That lady had favoured her with too many descriptions of how they had " up and down," " seeing and sawing," for Mrs. Dudley's heart to flutter at the prospect of wealth suddenly spread out before them.

" If it was here to-day, it was gone to-morrow," Mrs. Black had sadly lamented ; " and, while it was here, we had nothing but anxiety ; and when it was there, we had a trouble to keep the wolf from the door. I am sure, my dear, what I have gone through would make a history."

Heather Dudley not having the slightest desire to go through experiences sufficiently varied and unpleasant to justify any one compiling a history concerning her, would, had the choice been offered, decidedly have preferred remaining where there was no chance of such ups and downs as Mrs. Black mentioned occurring in her life.

The choice, however, not being offered, she had at last no alternative left but to bid adieu to Berrie Down; and, accompanied by Miss Hope, who kindly came up from Tunbridge Wells to "see the last" of her old favourite drive over to Palinsbridge, whence she travelled by one of the afternoon trains to London.

"I told you how it would be," said that Job's comforter, Alithea Hope, spinster, as she and Mrs. Dudley drove along the pleasant country roads to the station—Heather crouched up into one corner of Mrs. Seymour's carriage, so that her child might lie on the seat with her head resting on her mother's lap —"I told you how it would be, if you refused to take my advice; and now I hope you are satisfied at the result of your non-interference principle. Sweetness, and amiability, and submission, and all that kind of thing, are delightful traits, no doubt, in a wife, but they are qualities thrown away on Arthur Dudley—and so you will find out some day. The kindest thing you could have done to your husband would have been to say:

"'Now, look here, Arthur: if you are resolved to make a fool of yourself, I won't make a fool of myself with you. Go to town if you like, but I stay at Berrie Down. If you are determined to take the bread out of your children's mouths, I am equally resolved we shall not all be left paupers, if I can prevent it; therefore, I mean to remain and manage the farm, and whenever you are tired of your shares and your companies, and your Blacks and your town life, you can come home again.'"

Heather laughed; she was a little hysterical about leaving Berrie Down and all the kind friends she had recently found there, and so even while she laughed the tears came into her eyes again.

The idea of her making such a speech to Arthur; of her taking such a stand and setting her will up in open defiance of his; of her twitting her husband with his decision, and prophesying failure for him! Heather could not choose but laugh, and then she cried ; and then Miss Hope told her she was a soft, silly, stupid creature, who had no more business to marry Arthur Dudley than Mr. Raidsford had to marry that great vulgar illiterate dowdy, who " came over in her caravan to see you this morning ; you don't want me to speak about Mrs. Raidsford before Lally,—is that the meaning of all those signs ? The sooner Lally is taught to repeat nothing she hears, the better ; the sooner little girls learn their mouths and ears were given them to be kept tight shut, the more sugar-plums will be bought and popped in between their little red lips. Are you attending to me, Lally ?"

" Iss ; but how's me to eat sugar-plums if I keeps mows shut ?" inquired Miss Hope's pupil.

" You are to open it at proper times," answered her teacher ; " but not to repeat what older people say before you."

" Lally don't 'peat," replied the child, wearily. " Ma, is it far to London now ? will it be long before we are there ? me so tired—me so tired !"

Whereupon mother and aunt looked at each other, and Miss Hope said,—

" You will send for a doctor soon, Heather ; and

do try that delightful man I was speaking to you about. His manner with children is quite charming: wins their little hearts, and makes them feel at home with him directly. I am sure, when I went to him with Mrs. Walter Hope about her Charlie's legs, if he had been the boy's father he could not have taken more interest in his case; said he must see him at least once a week, for six months; took the child on his knee, and made himself so pleasant. There was only one stupid remark he made, which surprised me in so clever a man, namely, that he could tell in a moment whose child Charlie was, his likeness to his mother being remarkable. I longed to ask him where his eyes were, for the boy is a Hope, every inch of him, and very like me,—even his own father admits that."

Heather laughed again; she was evidently in a laughing mood, for the slightest thing provoked her merriment. Perhaps it was a comfort to this "silly goose" to discover that even Miss Hope had her weak points, and could be touched through them like her neighbours; perhaps the description of Charlie's model doctor tickled her fancy; any way she laughed; and Lally, putting up her little hand, patted her mother's cheek, and smiled a weak, faint smile in sympathy, while she asked,—

" Ma, was that 'tild as ill as me ?"

" Now I wonder," broke out Miss Hope, "if it be a consequence of 'original sin' that children always speak bad grammar. Is it the depravity of our human nature which always confounds the parts of speech, and makes a jumble of the personal pronouns? She never heard bad grammar spoken by any one belonging to her, and only listen to her English ; if you can call such a language as she speaks English. You want to know if Charlie was as ill as ' me,'" added the spinster, directly addressing Lally; "yes; and a great deal worse; his legs were like a bow, bent out like that;" and Miss Hope would have practically demonstrated what Charlie's legs were like on Lally's person, but that the child resisted any such experiments being attempted with her limbs. "Positively, Heather, you never saw such a sight as the child was," she continued ; "but Doctor Chickton assured Fanny he could make a perfect cure."

" Will he cure me ?" asked Lally, egotistical as most sick people are. Months of undivided materna solicitude, the devotion of a whole household, the visits of ladies vieing one with another who should bring Lally most toys and dainties, had spoiled the child a little, perhaps; or it may be that long illness and a close and undivided consideration of her own ailments, had produced a certain self-consciousness and absorption. In either case, there can be no question but that Lally was exceedingly sorry for herself, that she felt her case to be a very hard one; and that she was precisely in that state of mind and body which might well tire out any love except a mother's, any patience save that which seems well-nigh inexhaustible.

On the previous day Leonard and Lucy, and Cuthbert, together with Mrs. Piggott and Priscilla Dobbin, had journeyed to town, and now Heather and her first-born were bringing up the rear of the Dudley domestic army. It was a great point that Heather should have nothing to attend to excepting Lally, that she should not be troubled with luggage or parcels, or anything besides the sick child; and all the others being gone before, was a relief to her, so as to obviate the necessity for conversation or move-ment, or stir or sound, likely to disturb the little girl.

Mr. Plimpton, one of the most good-natured men who ever existed, saw Mrs. Dudley into her compartment, and impressed the guard with the importance of permitting no other passengers to intrude into it.

"The child is very ill indeed," he explained; which explanation he perhaps made clearer by slipping half-a-crown into the man's hand.

"I declare, if it were not that Lady Emily might wonder what had become of me, I would run up to town with you myself, Mrs. Dudley, and see you safe; but I think the guard will take care that no other passengers get in. Good-bye—good-bye, Miss Lally; don't quite forget me, though you are going to live in London. Have you any message for my wife? she will be certain to inquire whether you sent her one."

"Lally's love give her," said the child, who was now all excitement at the bustle, and the noise, and the steam, and the number of the people, and the general· variety,—"Lally's love—and a tiss;" and she kissed the tall gentleman, spite of his bushy whiskers and bristling moustache, both articles which ordinarily tried her equanimity and temper not a little.

"That child will never be better," was Mr. Plimpton's summary of Lally's state on his return home. "They may take her where they like, and send for whom they like, but she will never be strong again. Poor Mrs. Dudley believes it to be a question of treatment, but I am confident no treatment will ever put the little creature to-rights."

As for Miss Hope, she drove back to Berrie Down "crying like an idiot," so she informed Agnes all the way. "Dear me, I wish people would not have children," she said; "that Lally is enough to break a person's heart. Why cannot she get strong as any other child would? I declare I am out of patience with her, month after month, and like a bag of bones at the end. And of all things on earth she must set up a lamentation for that Bessie, whom she ought to have forgotten long ago; asking her mother if they should see her in London, and whether she would not be with them always, and sing to her at night. As if Heather were not vexed enough and sad enough without that;" and Miss Hope tossed aside her bonnet, which Laura carried up-stairs, for the spinster was going to stay with the girls for a time, to see how they went on and managed by themselves.

Then came a millennium of " Christian cookery," and of " coffee fit to be swallowed ;" then Miss Hope was in her element, — a mistress over two young mistresses, who obeyed her implicitly, and allowed her to order Susan about as much as she pleased.

But having one's own way is not always conducive to perfect happiness; being monarch of all one's surveys does not invariably produce perfect contentment. Even a contest with Mrs. Piggott would occasionally have served to break the monotony of being able to do as she pleased, which Miss Hope at length felt to be insupportable ; and every day, and a score of times during the course of every day, she repeated that Berrie Down was not Berrie Down without Heather, who, the guard proving faithful to the trust reposed in him, travelled alone to London with Lally, and was met at King's Cross by Alick and Lucy, the former of whom could only say, " Well, mother, this is a happy change for me," as he helped her out of the carriage, and walked beside her along the platform, carrying Lally in his arms.

There was no loneliness about that arrival in the great Babylon, even although Arthur could not meet his wife ;—for the strong hands which had smoothed

her way, and helped her through many a difficulty
at Berrie Down, were stretched forth now to guide
and guard her through the midst of the human
wilderness whither she had come.

CHAPTER XII.

NOT QUITE SATISFIED.

TIME went by once more; not as it had done at Berrie Down, smoothly as a calm river gliding noiselessly to the sea, but swiftly and excitedly, splashing among the stones, dashing between rocks, rushing over slight obstacles, eddying round larger impediments, rapid as a mountain stream speeding to the valley, with as great a roar and hurry and excitement as that wherewith water falls from a vast height into the basin it has through the centuries worn for itself below. Thus time sped by in London, so rapidly, so like an arrow cleaving the air, that often Heather's breath was almost taken from her by the swiftness and impetuosity of its passage.

And yet the change was not wholly or even

partially unpleasant.　There is a great adaptability about some natures which makes the work of transplantation easy and pleasant to accomplish.　Their roots are not ungrateful; move them where you will almost, they contrive to extract nourishment from the soil, and put forth their leaves, and their flowers, and their fruits, in the city, as in the field; in the midst of bricks and mortar, as away in the far country where the air is pure and pleasant.

They take good out of all things, whence good is possible to be extracted; they are willing to sing songs in a strange land, and will take down their harps and tune them in whatsoever household their lot is cast.　The man or woman who enjoys one pleasure keenly is not likely to be insensible to another;　and therefore, although Heather's first love was her last, still she made herself very contented in London—was amused with the excitement and the variety that surrounded her; went to concerts and theatres with all the pleasure a young girl might have evinced, and conducted herself, on the whole, not merely to the satisfaction of her husband, but also to that of Mr. Black.

Who was now a power not to be despised, a man

worth ever so much money, and likely to be worth ever so much more, a man engaged in floating fresh companies, and successful in obtaining grants and concessions, and first refusals, and early information to an extent which it would be quite outside the province of this story to explain more fully.

He had bought a splendid house out at Ealing, and was fitting it up regardless of expense. In Stanley Crescent he gave the most wonderful parties that it had ever entered into Mrs. Dudley's imagination to conceive could be given by any one not possessed of a ducal revenue. She had thought the furniture in Lincoln's Inn Fields far and away more expensive than any Mr. Black should have persuaded Arthur into purchasing, but the promoter assured her it was " all right ; upon his sacred word of honour, it had not cost a sixpence more than Dudley was perfectly justified in spending." And when she beheld Adamant House, as Mr. Black's new house at Ealing was happily called, she thought if one of the chiefs of the Company could afford such magnificence, their own, by comparison modest establishment, could not be considered " over-timbered," to quote from the promoter's vocabulary over again.

From room to room she walked, dazzled and bewildered, and Mr. Black walked beside, enjoying her astonishment, and kindly acting as cicerone to her inexperienced country understanding.

"Now, is not this better than grubbing on?" he triumphantly inquired, when, seated in his carriage, they were driving back to Lincoln's Inn. "This is what a man can do who is not afraid, who feels his own strength, and is sure of being able to keep his feet under him. Ay, and by Jove, Dudley shall do as well yet as I have done! He deserves to do well, and so do you, Mrs. Dudley; for a more sensible woman, and one less under the dominion of preju-dice, I never met. Many a wife would have striven to keep Dudley back—to dissuade him from coming to London, but you were too wise to attempt such interference, and therefore I say you deserve to succeed, and to have every bit as fine a carriage as this to bowl about in."

Which termination struck Heather as being so intensely ludicrous that she laughed outright, laughed even while she thought gravely enough that, had her interference been likely to produce the slightest good result, she would never have refrained from attempting it. This little explanation, however, being quite unnecessary to offer to Mr. Black, she took his compliment as though she deserved it every word, and laughed while the promoter thought, in his own elegant language, "that he had got to the blind side of Mrs. Dudley also, and would be shortly able to wind her round his finger as he had done the Squire."

In those early days, Arthur Dudley certainly proved himself to be as foolish and confiding a gentleman as any rogue need have desired to meet with.

Although he saw the grand house at Ealing, although every morning Mr. Black, *en route* to the City, thundered up to the door of the Protector Company's offices in his carriage and pair, and swaggered and blustered about the place as though the clerks, and the secretary, and the cashier, and the whole concern, in fact, were his own personal and exclusive property, still Arthur never insisted on a settlement of their accounts, never objected to renew bills, never made any difficulty about accepting new ones. He believed implicitly every sentence Mr. Black told him, and had much greater faith in the promoter's genius than in that of his own especial principal, Mr. Stewart, who, having put in a secretary and cashier of his own choosing, now rarely came near the office excepting on special board days, and when he paid formal visits to Mrs. Dudley, who always received him with the uncomfortable feeling, that if he knew who she really was, his calls would be fewer and shorter still.

But at length there came a certain coolness between the promoter and the secretary, which commenced in this wise:—

"Now I tell you what it is, Dudley," said Mr. Black, one day when, for the third time, his kinsman's renewals had been required and effected; "I tell you what it is,—this paper of yours has been through the fire often enough, it will never do to run it on till it gets scorched. You don't know what I mean, I see, but it is just this: a girl may walk out with a man once, and people think nothing about it—they may have met by accident, no consequence—but if she goes on walking, talk begins, there is some game up. Now, a man's credit is much in the same position. He may renew once or twice, and nobody thinks anything strange of his doing so; if he continue renewing, however, his name gets blown upon, and banks begin— especially if he be in no business—to look askance on his paper. That is your position at the present time; you must not ask for more discount, or, at least, if you do, you will not get it. I have done my best for you this time, and so has Crossenham, but I am greatly afraid we shall not be able to get you passed again."

"Then I suppose you will take up the bills next time?" suggested Arthur.

"I have no objection to taking up those that I have had value for," answered Mr. Black, a little astonished, perhaps, at Arthur's so speedily discovering the weak point in his armour; "but what are you to do with yours? That is the important part of the business, is it not?"

"I do not know," Arthur replied; "I should have supposed one part of it to be about as important as the other."

"Well, you would have supposed wrong, then," retorted Mr. Black; "because, though I am deucedly short, and shall be short for the next twelvemonth, still I could make a pinch of meeting my bills;

but how you are to take up yours, until the shares become marketable, I confess puzzles me to imagine —unless, indeed, you decide to raise a few thousands on Berrie Down."

"A few thousands!" repeated Arthur, in amazement, "a few thousands!   Why, my bills altogether cannot amount to more than a few hundreds!"

"Don't they, by Jove!" said Mr. Black, coolly. "Just run your eye over that little list—there is not sixpence of mine among it,—and you will soon change your opinion.   You have had a lot of money, one time and another.   Then you bought this place; then there is the discount."

"I thought you were going to pay that?" Arthur interrupted.

"On those which were drawn for my accommodation, of course," replied Mr. Black.   "I am now talking of yours.   Then there was the doing up of this house——"

"You told me the Company would put it in proper order for me to live in," once again interposed Mr. Dudley.

"So they would, had it been for any other person excepting the owner of the house," answered Mr.

Black. "I had, as I told you, to waive that point. I wrote you all about it after you were up at the beginning of the year."

"Indeed, you are mistaken," said Arthur ; "you never wrote a syllable to me on the subject!"

"All I can say is, then, that I either wrote or intended to write," answered Mr. Black ; "but I had such a deuce of a lot of things to attend to about that time, your letter may have slipped my memory. However, that's nothing to do with what we are talking of now. If you will consider the affair, it was absurd to expect the Company both to pay you rent and to paint and paper your house. They could not do it. I forgot about its being your own property—about your, in fact, being landlord and our being tenants, till you were back at Berrie Down. We pay you a very good rent, so you must not be dissatisfied. Then, you see, there is the furniture."

"Good Heavens!" exclaimed Arthur, "you never mean to say that the furniture we have in this house cost twelve hundred and seventy-eight pounds? Where could twelve hundred and seventy-eight pounds worth be put?"

"My dear fellow, how you talk!" said Mr. Black, with a smile of infinite superiority, "why, you might put double the money up in a corner and scarcely see it! Most economical I call the whole arrangement. You have a drawing-room fit to ask anybody into, a grand trichord thingumygig of Erard's, good solid chairs and tables, every room fully carpeted, dinner and dessert services complete, glasses large enough for Buckingham Palace, bed-chambers that you need not mind putting a duke to sleep in —all for twelve hundred odd pounds!"

"But that is more than a year's income," Arthur persisted.

"I beg your pardon—taking rent and everything, it is not nearly a year's income; but, even if it were, the man who can rig a house up like this for a twelve months' pay, is a very fortunate fellow. I told you, I would not run you to a farthing's unnecessary expense, and neither I did. In your position here, in London, it would not do for you to have the same old-fashioned curiosities that served your purpose very well at Berrie Down; besides, the money is not lost, there is the furniture—well kept, it would fetch its cost any day by auction; now tot up those items, and let us see the sum total. Yes; that is just what I made it, running through the account roughly—four thousand six hundred and eleven pounds, seventeen shillings and nine pence."

"Mr. Black! I never had that sum of money," said Arthur, excitedly.

"If you had not money, you had goods," answered Mr. Black; "but you have had a smartish sum of money too. The pace you have gone at the last twelvemonth has not been a slow one. Those dinners you gave—and the money you spent town——"

"But you said the Company would pay all that."

"So it has; you have your shares and your salary, and your good rent for these premises. I never meant direct payment. The idea is absurd. How would an entry like this sound :

" 'Dinner at the Wellington, to six desirable City men,' or 'Treating Cadger's managing clerk to the theatre, with supper after,' or 'Stall tickets to the Misses Smithers,' or 'Half a sov. to Jenkins' footman!' Just bring the thing home, Dudley; think how ridiculous it would sound, and don't be unreasonable. You have had your penn'orths, and you will have more—besides, it really is this house and furniture, neither of which is likely to run away, that has walked into the money. Think over the matter, will you? any time during the course of the next two months, and let me know what you decide;" and with that, the promoter was airily taking himself out of the room, when "Black!" sharply spoken by his companion, arrested his departure.

"I never had this money," Mr. Dudley repeated. "I never could have had it; where has it gone—what has been done with it?"

"As for that, Dudley," was the reply—"take my advice, and never waste your time inquiring after spent money. Enough for you, or any man, to know that it has gone—to the tomb of all those people one hears about. No use trying to hold a *post-mortem* examination on the body of a defunct ten-pound note. For the rest, you both could and did have all the sums I have debited you with; they are regularly entered on their dates of payment in my books. First day you are down in the City, call in and check them off. I'd rather you would do so—more satisfactory for us both."

And with this Parthian shot, Mr. Black said "Good-day," and shut the office-door after him, leaving Arthur far too much perplexed and bewildered to consider that a lie can be written as well as spoken, any day in the year, and that the mere fact of an entry to his debit being made on such and such a date, did not by any means of necessity prove that such debt had ever been incurred.

END OF VOL. II.

LONDON: PRINTED BY WILLIAM CLOWES AND SONS STAMFORD STREET AND CHARING CROSS.

www.ingramcontent.com/pod-product-compliance
Lightning Source LLC
Chambersburg PA
CBHW020925120726
47905CB00008B/2393